Catholic School Boys

Catholic School Boys

Robert R. Bell

Cawing
Crow
Press

Published by:

Cawing Crow Press LLC

Dunlo, PA

ISBN: 978-1-68264-001-2

Library of Congress Control Number: 2015953560

Visit us on the web at: www.cawingcrowpress.com

Prologue

I read in the local newspaper this morning that old Saint Matthew decided to close his doors for good. I thought it was noteworthy but certainly not unexpected. The school had to cease operations for the usual reasons: declining attendance, crumbling buildings, bleak finances. I'm not sure why this put me in a melancholy mood. For better or worse, it fixated my mind on the distant past—to my days at Saint Luke.

When I began my studies at that venerable institution in Nineteen Sixty-seven—still in its heyday, there were a total of ten Catholic schools situated in our small town. By the time I began my final year at Saint Luke in September, Nineteen Seventy-four, there were just seven schools still in business—mostly because of consolidation, and our high school had disbanded a few years earlier. With Saint Matt deciding to call it quits, there are now none.

I could never imagine such a thing happening back in the old days—a time when my parents insisted that I was to be educated in a Catholic school, and most of my friend's parents felt the same. At the very least, it raised a question or two...or three. Are there fewer Catholics today? Are people less concerned or less dedicated regarding their faith? Or...are there simply less hypocrites then there used to be?

After a little bit of research, I discovered that it wasn't just a local phenomenon but an obvious trend everywhere. I refer to it as the *collapse of the Catholic school system;* the reasons not being certain. Although, after all of these years, I'm still torn between considering my final year at Saint Luke as the most significant year of my life—or what should be the most forgettable.

On the positive side, it's where I learned the most about friendship and where I first discovered love...in an odd way. I may have been shown the meaning of life, or at least the importance of testing my faith about god. I learned plenty of other lessons too, albeit usually the hard way. But there was also perversion, violence and sin of all kinds everywhere I looked. I wasn't just from my fellow students, but it was from some of our superiors as well. It was indeed a confusing time.

My thoughts would often reflect back on some of those involved: the sinister Father Spencer, the gay and sadistic teacher— (Uncle) Joe Knight, the heavy handed and unpredictable Penguins (nuns), the seductive Cathy, the notorious Santino brothers, the dimwitted, free spirited Ratboy—my best pal, and others. At the very least, it was an interesting era filled with many colorful characters and surprising events. Maybe sometimes we have to take the good with the bad. Perhaps it's all part of the plan —this process of educating thyself

Chapter One

September Seventy-four

It was just the second day back to school, and the action was already heating up. We were the eighth graders — the senior class — at Saint Luke, and we were going to make it a memorable year regardless of the obstacles that were in store for us.

The two-thirty bell rang. Thank God! Sister Mary Catherine's Religion class was a real snoozer, just like it always had been, but the last thing you wanted to do was doze off during her lecture. She would sneak up on you and scream a high pitch in your ear.

Before I got out of my seat, I noticed that my best friend, Chucky Dalton, had hurried out of the room. I walked out into the hallway and saw that he was hustling toward the exit door. He was just as recognizable from the back as he was from the front with his unkempt hair and soiled, worn, barely white dress shirt.

"Ratboy — wait up! Hold up, Chuck!" I called

He just kept going. It seemed like he was ignoring me. I watched him and his worn out, untied Keds as he ducked and weaved his way down the long hallway that led to the front doors. He managed to get past the other students who were beginning to pour out from their classroom without hitting into any of them.

I chased after him thinking that he might fall on his face again just like he always did. I caught up to him, and together we raced toward the school's exit. We pushed open both doors, and were greeted by the warm, late summer sunshine. It hit my face and reminded me of the freedom we had all summer long.

As soon as I made it outside, he started to run again. I repeated, "Ratboy—wait up! Hold up, Chuck! Your shoe's untied!"

This time he turned toward me while trying to catch his breath. I was a little annoyed and asked, "What the heck are you running for? What's going on?"

"I don't want to miss the fight." He bent down and tied his shoe laces.

"What fight? What are you talking about?"

"Marty Monday and Mike Santino. They talked about it all summer long. Where the hell have you been?"

"I didn't hear anything. I just ran past Marty in the hall, and I saw Mike go into the bathroom. Are you sure about this?"

"I want to get there before they do. You'll see—come on." Ratboy headed for the alley that ran behind the schoolyard.

The road had not been paved in years and was pockmarked with small and large potholes that we had to dodge when running, or else we could twist our ankles. On the school side it was blocked form view by a line of boxwood hedges that had grown up over ten-feet tall and was lined on the other side by the garages of the houses that were on the next block over. Back here we were invisible. That's why it was designated as the schools official fight ring. There were many classic slugfests that had happened on this sacred ground, and new legends were being born every year.

We usually got past the first week without much violence, but I had a feeling that it was going to be different this year. One way or the other, we all wanted to leave our mark for posterity, and an historic brawl was one sure way to do it.

Ratboy was the first spectator to arrive, followed by me, and then a group of girls from the sixth, seventh, and eighth grades. Most of the girls in the school didn't seem to be as squeamish as one might think. No, they actually seemed to be drawn to the violence as much as any of the boys...maybe even more so. As a matter of fact, they may have been placing bets.

In a matter of minutes, there were at least fifty of us eagerly awaiting the arrival of the two gladiators. There was laughing, yelling, pushing, and shoving. I thought that another fight would breakout in the crowd before the main event would begin.

Mike Santino was the first brawler to arrive, and he was accompanied by his younger brother Tony. There were three Santino brothers attending Saint Luke. They all had reputations for toughness…or at least cockiness. This was something that was instilled by their dad, *Angelo* before they even made it to first grade. Angelo Santino was rumored to be a hitman for the mob. Nobody dared to mess around with *Big Angelo*.

Mike, with his dark curly hair and piercing blue eyes just stood there with his teeth and fists clenched, while waiting for Mighty Marty to show up.

I'd witnessed Mike in a few scraps in the past, but I had yet to see Marty demonstrate his fighting skills. I heard that he got into a brawl on the fourth of July, and that his opponent had lost a tooth. Of course, the only proof I had of this were the words that came from the mouth of Ratboy. He said that he had heard about it from someone else. I think they call that hearsay in court, and it was less likely to be believed since Ratboy was so gullible himself. You could tell him the sky was orange and he would believe you. Marty just happened to be the biggest kid in the school, and he could possibly be the best player on the basketball team for the upcoming season, which certainly didn't hurt his standing. So, I could almost believe the tooth story.

We waited for about twenty-minutes, and the crowd that had now grown to nearly one-hundred grew more and more restless with every passing minute.

I heard a voice behind me whisper, "Marty chickened out."

Another voice said, "I saw him sneak out of the back entrance of the school. Coward!"

I didn't want to believe it, but maybe there wouldn't be a big fight after all, or perhaps Mike would just pick someone out of the crowd to square off with. That would have been fine with me, as long as I wasn't the one that was singled out.

Mike had a disappointed yet somewhat relieved expression on his face. His brother and corner man — Tony, who was a skinnier and less intimidating version of his brother, tapped him on the shoulder and said, "That pussy went home. He chickened out. We'll kick his ass tomorrow."

About a minute later, just when everyone started leaving, a tall figure approached from the opposite end of the alley. It was Marty! Perhaps he needed time to build up his courage, or he got held after school by the penguins (that's what we called the priests and nuns because of the black and white garb they wear). He approached Mike with a confident look on his face. When he was about ten-feet away, he stopped, and the big stare down ensued. Mike had the thousand mile stare going, while Marty's face was more relaxed, as if he had seen it all before.

The crowd gradually separated into two groups. About half of the audience was now standing behind Mike, and the other half was behind Marty. I stood off to the side. I happened to be friendly with both of them and didn't want to make any new enemies. Then again, I was everyone's friend. I didn't want to take sides. I just wanted to either be liked...or left alone.

All of a sudden, I heard Ratboy's stupid voice yelling, "Kick his ass, Marty!" It was quickly followed by a dirty look that Mike peered back toward him. I knew what that meant. Ratboy would get his own beating later on. Whether we were inside the school or outside of it, Chuck would always have difficulty learning his lessons.

Both brawlers just stood there speechless. Finally, Mike initiated the first shove. Marty followed with a hefty push of his own. After a few more shoves, Marty put Mike in a headlock. Both combatants fell on the ground and were attempting to choke the life out of each other. The crowd was mostly silent the whole time, except for an occasional outburst from someone that was pretending to root for one of the pugilists. Although, nobody really cared who would win, except for those who had bets on it.

Eventually, they broke free of each other's grip, and then quickly got back on their feet. That's when the first punch was thrown. It was a solid connection just below Marty's left eye, and he appeared dazed.

He was cut!

A small amount of blood started to trickle down his cheek. Then it turned to a flow. It was an ugly shade of red. It made me cringe. Maybe it was because I didn't like red. My mom decorated everything in our house in red. I never knew why. I especially hated those ugly red curtains she had hung in the living room.

I just stood there in a mild state of shock. I had seen my share of fights over the years. I was even in one of my own in sixth grade — sort of. I didn't actually hit my opponent. It was just a feeble attempt at wrestling. This was the first time that I had ever seen someone bleed like that. I saw it on television a few times but not in real life. Besides, we were just kids. I thought that you had to be an adult to bleed that much after being hit, or maybe if you were shot like my uncle was in Vietnam.

Just then, I saw one of the male teachers along with two of the penguins coming toward us. Marty and most of the other kids decided to scatter. Mike, Ratboy, and I decided to stay put. The male teacher was Joe Knight, who was an unfair and miserable man that almost everyone hated. I happened to be in an extremely awkward position because Mr. Knight just happened to be Uncle Joe to me.

He was accompanied by Sister Theresa and the principal— Sister Ann Margaret. We all took a step back when Uncle Joe approached us. He was rather intimidating with his craggy face, shiny white hair, and his offensive breath that smelled like a mixture of dirty socks and three-day old onions.

They were three of the school's biggest disciplinarians, and we all knew, way too well, how it felt to have our egos and asses bruised. On the plus side, it was only the second day of school, and the SS Squad still had their semi-friendly, welcoming faces on. The beatings, deep knee bends, cleaning the blackboards, and writing ten thousand times—*I will be a good Catholic boy*—usually didn't happen until later in the semester.

Uncle Joe and his two henchwoman took a minute to stare us down. Even though Sister Ann Margaret was the official head of the school, she often let Uncle Joe take control of the *hooligans*, as she called us. He was the most dominant force within the confines of Saint Luke. Some might say that he had certain sadistic values— among other issues that made him fit right in.

We stood there in silence looking at our fates as they seemed to be sizing us up for our punishments.

Uncle Joe finally spoke. "Okay, what is going on here? What are you three up to?"

Mike, Ratboy, and I looked at each other nervously without saying a word.

"Come on—out with it!" He insisted.

The three of us—using our best *poor* grammar uttered to our annoyed English teacher, "Uh…uh…no…we ain't doing nuthin, Mr. Knight."

I referred to him as Mr. Knight, partly because I was embarrassed that he was my not so Great Uncle, but mostly because he wouldn't have it any other way. I got no favoritism thrown toward me. Well, maybe he didn't have me on his radar screen as much as some of the others, but that was because he probably didn't like getting too many phone calls from my dear, protective mom—his favorite niece.

He then gave us a look like he wanted to simultaneously crack the three of us in the face—like Moe, Larry, and Shemp, but he didn't. Instead, he just pointed and said, "Okay—clear out…and brush up on your grammar. I'll see you bums tomorrow."

The three of us headed down the long alleyway that always seemed to be darkened from the shade of the garages and hedges lining the sides. I took the lead. Ratboy and Mike were right behind me…at least I thought they were.

I heard a thud! I turned around and saw Ratboy lying on the ground, and Mike was kicking him in the head and stomach. I should have done something when I saw my best pal covering up in pain, but Mike was my friend too…I think. Besides, he was just as intimidating to me as Uncle Joe—well, almost.

When Mike grew tired of kicking the crap out of Ratboy, he looked at me and said, "See you tomorrow, Tom." Then he simply walked away like it was just a usual routine for him while poor Ratboy was still lying in the fetal position on the ground.

I guess that Mike didn't like the fact that Ratboy was rooting for Marty and then tried to suck up to him after he unofficially won the fight. On the other hand, Ratboy seemed to get beatings from just about everyone for every reason imaginable. He even stopped wearing underwear because of all the wedgies that he had received over the years.

I helped lift him off the ground while he coughed and held his hand over his aching stomach. "Come on Chuck. Let's just go home now."

As we walked away, neither of us said anything about what had just occurred. Instead, we just started crooning to the songs of our generation—the music of our lives. Actually, I crooned, and he painfully moaned along with me. We couldn't remember most of the words to "Seasons in the Sun", "Spiders and Snakes", and "Billy Don't be a Hero." Then we fouled up the words to the "No No Song" and "Hooked on a Feeling" so bad that we started to just make up our own.

We walked up to the top of Mannicort Hill. There were old blood stains, glass from broken wine bottles, and cigarette butts that were littering the sidewalk. We usually got a little nervous when we went past one run-down old home that we dubbed—*the hippie house.* There were usually strange sounds and odd smells that came flowing out of its windows, and there were always three or more motorcycles parked in the driveway. I remembered seeing raunchy looking men with long beards and tattoos hanging around. They wore leather vests that read *Chosen Few* on the back. I remembered thinking that possibly it was a religious thing, and that maybe they attended Saint Luke at one time. I guess that wasn't the case though, because I was reminded by several concerned parents to just stay away!

It was a long uphill walk through a seedy part of town for both of us. When we got to the point where we usually parted ways, Ratboy stuck out his hand for the customary—slap me five! His hands always looked dirty for some reason, but I still couldn't resist. He continued his journey up another hill to the highest point in town—the dreaded Terrace Projects. It was populated with wayward youth and degenerates of all ages. I was a little more fortunate. I lived one street below that zoo.

I stood there watching as Ratboy walked up into the sky, and I waited to see if one of the rowdy slum kids would jump out of the bushes to ambush and pulverize him. It was an event that I had already witnessed on two other occasions. I also started wondering why I would pick such an unlikely candidate as Charles —Ratboy— Dalton to be my best friend. He did have a catchy name though… *that is if he was a criminal.*

Chuck was unattractive, unintelligent, unpopular, and he excelled at nothing. I didn't excel at anything either, but I just managed to blend in a lot better than he ever could. I didn't think that he deserved to be beaten up as much as he was, but there something about him. It was like there was an aura that radiated from inside his body that made people want to pound him. Maybe it was because he looked like he needed it. Maybe they were just bored and they needed to work out on a punching bag, and he kind of resembled one. He was ninety-nine dirty pennies for a dollar.

Having a nickname like Ratboy certainly didn't help his case, and I'll admit that I was the guilty party that stuck him with that label. It just came naturally to me a few years back when we were in the lunch room. He was eating a piece of cheese when I noticed that his ears were too big and pointy for a normal human being's and that he had way too much body hair for a kid his age. The way he nibbled on that cheese with his pointy ears and hairy body reminded me of a rat.

One thing for sure was that there wasn't anyone on this earth more durable than he was. If the nuns or Uncle Joe weren't beating him in the school, his fellow students were nailing him outside of Fort Saint Luke. The project kids made an example of him, and there was his drunken, abusive father who beat him on a regular basis.

I was much more fortunate. I could count on one hand how many times I got my clock cleaned by teachers, parents, or other kids…well, maybe part of my second hand too. Still, I considered myself to be one of the *chosen few*.

When Chuck disappeared from my view, I began to walk down the middle of my long and narrow, cobblestone street to reach my house. The further I got down the block, the nicer the neighborhood became, mostly because everything was so familiar to me after having walked down the street a thousand times before. I thought about everything that I had already witnessed during the first two days of school. Most of it was about what I had expected it to be:

annoying nuns, Uncle Joe, discipline, basketball, candy store, Ratboy, Mike, Marty, and...*girls?*

I noticed that Cathy Davis and Jane Adams breasts had grown. They didn't have them in seventh grade…at least I didn't recall seeing any. Veronica Dorsey had them since second grade. Hers looked as big as beach balls. Their skirts seemed to be a little shorter than they were in seventh grade too. Maybe all the girls had gotten taller, and they were still wearing the same skirts from the last year.

No more than two inches above the knees – girls.

Cathy totally ignored that rule. Hers were at least four inches above…maybe five…even six?

Okay, I got a shot of her rose colored underwear when she uncrossed her legs during religion class. I think that she knew it, but she wasn't embarrassed. I was—just a little. I know that I felt awfully warm and fuzzy in the head. It was a different type of feeling—a new experience for me.

Mike told me that he once saw what was beneath Cathy's underwear after the school dance last year—liar! He told me that it was an ugly site—liar! Liar! I would rather find out for myself. Besides, does he think his is pretty? Not from my point of view when I snuck a peak before he went into the shower after a basketball game the last season. I didn't tell him though. I knew that he would have killed me if I did.

How did Mike grow hair down there already? I still didn't have any. Even Ratboy, who had hair growing out of his ears, didn't, and he was a year older than the rest of us—or maybe two years? That's because Ratboy was held back, or maybe his parents forgot to register him or something. I wonder if Cathy had any hair. I should ask Mike—liar! Liar! Liar!

All of my thinking about that nonsense, and not paying attention to where I walked, was why part of the three inch heel of one of my platform shoes got caught in the crevice of a manhole cover. I tripped, while twisting my ankle and fell in the middle of the street. I looked around and saw that nobody was around to witness it. My smooth reputation was still intact—thank Jesus!

I looked way to cool to be caught tripping in the middle of the street. Saint Luke decided to do away with the standard Neo-Nazi uniform by the time I made it to seventh grade, and that was fine by me. They were tired of losing attendance to the public schools where the kids could wear any clothes that they pleased.

Saint Luke decided to give in a little to the changing times. I could wear what I wanted, as long as it wasn't sneakers, jeans, or t-shirts. We still had to wear a tie though. I never learned how to make the knot properly, so I cheated and used a fakey—a clip-on that I snatched off every chance I got.

I dressed better than my pals did. I didn't shop at Mortin's Discount Mart like most of them. My folks let me buy my threads at

Sonny's Sport Shop. My flared pants and balloon sleeve shirts were colorful, and some of my threads sparkled! Because of the price, I could only get a few new outfits a year, so I had to rotate every three or four days. I would still rather have three sets of Sonny's stuff over six of Martin's duds. Most of poor Ratboy's clothes were secondhand. They were handed down from his older brother or sometimes his *sister*.

The school wasn't quite as lenient with the girls. Even though they did away with the old standards, they still had to wear a *nice Catholic girl skirt*. The skirts did seem to have gotten shorter…and thinner…and…oops; I almost tripped again.

I was just about to my front gate, and my thoughts were back to the music. I thought about Gilbert O'Sullivan's, "Alone Again (Naturly)" for some reason, and I started to incorrectly sing those lyrics.

No, that song is already a couple years old, I thought. I needed to get back to the top forty. Then I spotted an eight legger crawling on the ground in front of me. He was trying to live out his final days, but I ended his misery with an exaggerated heel stomp. Then I instinctively went into my own lyrics, "I never liked spiders—and that ain't what Cathy needs to like me…uh…uh…." While I sang I felt like I was simultaneously hearing the nuns reciting…*School boys, school boys, little Catholic school boys.*

I snapped out of it when I heard the four o'clock church bell chime. I thought that I might do my homework before dinner. "Shit!" I just then realized that I didn't have it with me. I ran out of Sister Mary Catherine's class so fast when I chased Ratboy that I didn't realize that I had left it all on my desk. I walked into my house by the time the fourth bell rang, and I just kept singing—"I never liked Spiders...I like Cathy Davis...School boys...All alone again...Shit!"

Chapter Two

Next Day

I got up earlier than usual the next morning. My mom didn't even have to raise her voice for once. I had so many pleasant, and just as many unpleasant, thoughts that were occupying my brain that I could hardly get a restful night's sleep. I was always told that no matter what happens Saint Luke would watch over me from above and all around. Now, if he failed for some reason, there was always my mom, the nuns, Jesus, Uncle Joe, and Ratboy, but not necessarily in that order.

I wanted to be the first kid to make it to school so that I wouldn't miss out on any of the happenings. I wanted to hear the rumors and possibly start one of my own. Saint Luke was almost a mile from my house, but most of it was downhill. I could make it from my doorstep to the school building in five minutes flat if I had to, and I needed to on many occasions in the past. I made it out the door by seven-thirty. Today, there was no need to hurry.

Sometimes, Ratboy would wait for me on the steps above Mannicort Hill, but I didn't see him, or anyone else, as I made my way toward Saint Luke. When I made it to the imposing, black, iron entrance gate to the school, I noticed that two kids had already gotten there before me. I thought that it was a strange coincidence when I saw it was Mike and Marty. It looked like a possible parley in the corner of the schoolyard.

The two bruisers saw me enter the gate. As I approached them, I wasn't sure which one I wanted to greet first. I just nodded to both of them and kept walking. They seemed to be involved in some heavy negotiations. Their faces were really close to each other; it almost looked like they were about to kiss. I thought they might start fighting again. I was ready to be the only spectator for the main event. What a story I would have, but they backed away from each other and continued their conversation. Mike did most of the talking, so I decided to walk past them and head into the school. Besides, I didn't feel that I would be able to contribute much to their conversation, nor would they want to hear it anyway.

As I walked past that dynamic duo, Mike said to Marty, "Okay, I'll work my side of the yard and you'll work yours."

Marty was a boy-man of few words. He usually only talked when he felt that he needed to. He just responded with, "Right on."

But what did it all mean? I pondered it. Did it mean that they were going to try to control all of the inmates' activities in the yard?

Would they shake down the younger and weaker kids for their milk money? Would they put a mark on one of the penguins? Whatever they were scheming, I doubt if Saint Luke would have approved, and I knew for damn sure that Uncle Joe wouldn't.

Saint Luke was always watching us from the ancient murals and plaques that bore his face which decorated several places on the outside of the building—and a few on the inside too. Uncle Joe chose to watch us from a little window on the third floor—like the warden of an institution. He was probably still naïve enough to think that we never noticed that he was there. We would sometimes say—*Oh brother is watching you.*

Mike Santino was much too dramatic. He watched way too much television and went to the movies every weekend. His parents bought him some kind of remote control device that allowed him to change channels without getting off of the couch. He spent a lot of time with his dad too. The Don even took Mike with him to see The Godfather when he was only in sixth grade. I remembered hearing that part two was coming out soon. I was sure he would see that one too. It wasn't hard to imagine how Mike would turn out.

I needed to stay focused. My main mission for that morning was to sneak into Sister Mary Catherine's classroom, grab the homework off of my desk, and try to make quick work of my assignment. I didn't want to start the year off on the wrong toe, like I did in seventh grade…and sixth…and…oh—forget it.

I imagined that I was a secret agent on a dangerous assignment. I tiptoed up to the entrance way. I peered through the stained glass, which I always thought was kind of odd for the school to use on the entrance door. I was told that they had some of it left over from when they refurbished the church a few years back. They didn't want to waste it, and it kind of made the school look, well...more holy.

I pulled open the door. It made a loud creaking sound, one that I had never seemed to notice before. It looked almost too dark inside like the sun hadn't come up yet. Saint Luke was big on conservation: minimal lighting, no air conditioning, and a heating system that only seemed to work in January and February after the frost from our breath would fill up the classroom. The school had always looked run down to me, yet the cost of tuition still went up every year.

Our parents got a letter—like clockwork at the beginning of every August. It would mention the need for the increase. It was a different excuse every year. The most recent letter mentioned an increase in transportation costs. In other words, Father Spencer was due for a new Cadillac. The year before, they mentioned legacy cost, which I later found out meant that they had to hire more civilian teachers because less new nuns were entering the fray.

Traditionally speaking, the Sisters were considered to be cheap labor, and they were provided housing via the convent. It didn't seem like much money went into the old school, so someone must have been skimming the pot. It wasn't a secret that they would make a killing at the church bazaars from the brainless gamblers at the poker, dice, and spinning wheel tables. I thought about all of this as I caught a quick sip from my favorite drinking fountain. I wondered if some day they might try to bottle the cheap water and sell it to us too.

I started to gracefully trot down the hallway by using just the balls of me feet. I was able to make good time while producing minimal noise. When I made it to Sister Mary Catherine's classroom, I turned on the light and noticed that my writing tablet and a few books were just where I had left them. I started to giggle softly as I gathered the evidence from my desk. Then I turned and started to make my way out of the room while glancing at the notes that I had written down in my tablet. When I looked up, guess who stood there blocking the door?

Well, I think it was…but she didn't look the part. She wasn't wearing her habit, or the usual headdress for that matter. She let down her hair. She was basically in street clothes. She was a wide woman. She didn't even look like a nun at that moment. She looked more like a man—like a football linebacker or somebody. The combination between the warm morning air, running down the hall, and not having any idea what to say made me sweat the same way I did when I was playing basketball outside on a hot July afternoon.

She didn't say anything either. She seemed to be totally out of character—as well as uniform. I cautiously approached her and took a big swallow. "Good morning Sister Mary Catherine. I…uh…forgot my homework yesterday. I wanted to get it done before class started."

I had to say something, even though I still wasn't one-hundred percent certain that it was her.

When I got about a foot away from where she stood firm like a sumo wrestler, she grabbed me under my two armpits, hoisted my skinny ass into the air, and slammed me into the blackboard. She sniffed at me like I smelled bad or maybe it was something else. She examined me in a way that made me feel like I was her prey. Then, to my surprise, she finally managed, "You're not going to give me any shit this year—are you, Mr. Richards?"

"No, Sister…I…uh…no…I won't. I promise I won't." I looked down at my feet dangling in the air, and I knew that I didn't have the nerve to kick her in the balls, or where they would have been.

She was still waiting for more out of me. I had to give her something else, and I suddenly had a vision in my head of her slapping Ratboy around. I said nervously, "I told Chucky Dalton that he needs to show more respect to you this year. He promised that he would." It was a wonderful lie.

The big brute held me for a few seconds longer. Then she gave me a wink and lowered me back to the ground. She didn't say anything about the homework. She started to head out of the room. "See you at seventh period, Mr. Richards." My ass kissing had saved me once again.

It was just the first week of school, and I had already experienced some pretty interesting shit. I wondered if Sister Mary

Catherine had been waiting for me, or if it was just another coincidence.

It would be surprising to me if she had intentionally allowed me to see her without her customary attire. It was one hell of an ugly sight too. I just hoped that she didn't make a *habit* out of it.

As I made my way out of her classroom, I thought about something that she told us while we were in class a few years back. She said that she came from a strict Roman Catholic family. She told us that when she was growing up, it was expected that one child from every such family would enter into the priesthood, the sisterhood, or some-hood. She also said that she had only one sibling and that he was mentally challenged. I guess that meant that she didn't have much of a choice. I also felt that perhaps Sister Mary Catherine didn't love her job and that she may have several vices. I started to visualize her doing other types of work: bar bouncer, lumberjack, Marine. I daydreamed way too much, especially when I was inside her tired classroom.

I headed down the hallway to get out of the building where it was safer…maybe? When I got to the front steps, Jane Adams stood there all alone. She was arguably the cutest girl in my class, and I always felt that she outclassed me by a mile. Besides, she'd been on Mike Santino's radar screen for some time now.

I noticed that Mike looked over at us when Jane began to speak to me. "Cathy Davis thinks you're cute, Tom."

"Who…me? She said that? Really?"

"Yea…she said that you tried to look up her skirt too."

"No…no—no—It was an accident. I…uh…uh…just happen to be looking at uh…." I didn't know what to say. I started sweating again.

Then she asked, "Why is your face so red? Are you sick or something? What's wrong with you?"

"I don't know. I'm…part Indian, I think?"

I immediately regretted confessing my heritage. I was told that I was a tiny bit Cherokee on my mom's side. I never admitted it to anyone before. I wasn't exactly proud of it. There were no Indians in my school, and I didn't want to be teased about it.

Then she decided to pry further. "I heard that Mr. Knight is your uncle. I think that's pretty weird."

I was even less proud of that. I tried to keep it a secret for years, but I knew that everyone would eventually find out about it. I was embarrassed by my unfortunate circumstances, and I'm sure that my face got even redder. "Yea, I heard he was related to me too." What a stupid thing to say, I immediately thought. Of course, he is related to me.

She started to giggle, and then she asked, "Is he also part Indian then?"

"I don't know what he is. We are barely related. He's like a distant uncle or something."

I sometimes wished that Uncle Joe was a lot more distant. He was often close enough that you could sense his awful breath. I was desperate to come up with something cool to say to Jane, but I kept striking out.

Before I got a chance to make a hit, Mike made his way over to us. He looked at me first with an unfriendly expression, and then he broke into a smile when he looked at her and said semi-sweetly, "Hi, Jane. What's up?"

"Hi, Mike. I was telling Tom that Cathy likes him, and he told me that he was an Indian."

At that moment I wished that I would have stayed inside of the building. A few seconds later, the eight-thirty bell rang to let all the little Catholic boys and girls know that they had five minutes to sit up straight at their desks before all the doors were closed and locked. Jane skipped her way up the steps. Mike and I were right behind her. Our eyes were fixated on her long slender legs.

Mike didn't say anything about the Indian comment. But he had plenty to say about a certain female. "Did you know she was a slut? She let me finger her over the summer. Tony played with it a little bit too."

I could hardly believe that he would talk about classy Jane Adams that way. I just responded with, "What? Who are you talking about?"

"Cathy Davis. Who did you think I'm talking about?"

I hated at least half of the filth that came out of Mike's mouth, but as usual I was passive about it.

As we walked into the building, I realized that I forgot all about the reason that I got there so early in the first place. My mind was a ball of confusion that easily got sidetracked most of the day. The best thing I had going for me was that I seemed to be liked by just about everyone. It was hard not to like me. I knew how to fit in. I didn't take sides either. I didn't know how to argue. In a school that was full of bullies of every possible size, shape, age, and gender, I just naturally learned how to dance, unlike Ratboy who seemed to have two left feet.

As soon as we got inside the building, Mike started to wave his hand back and forth toward his mouth while stomping on the floor and making sounds to imitate an Indian. I knew that I wouldn't get away with it. He told some of the other kids, and I was harassed all day long.

Even the jovial Sister Helen—the History teacher— caught wind of the gag and got in to the imitating Indian act right in front of the entire class. She even had the nerve to call on me during a discussion about George Washington crossing the Delaware River. She smiled at me and said, "How?"

I just sat there thinking that Saint Luke looked down on it all in shame. Maybe it was just another coincidence on a day that was destined to be full of them. Maybe I was just too sensitive, but it sure felt like it was intentional. I wasn't sure of the answer that she was looking for, so I just stupidly blurted out, "An Indian canoe?"

The entire class erupted in laughter. Sister Helen laughed the loudest and kept pointing at me. I could only imagine how red my face must have looked at that point. She never told me if my answer was right. Instead, she went into her silly little rain dance again.

Twice in the same day I had witnessed some inappropriate behavior by two of the most senior nuns in the school. I was often amazed regarding the character of some of the individuals that were there to educate and discipline us. There must have been a penguin shortage everywhere, except for maybe…Antarctica.

Was it the beginning of the end? The attendance level dropped every year. I wondered if it would have made a difference if I would have attended the public school. Saint Luke had disbanded its high school a few years earlier. That meant that I would be attending Rockwood my final four years anyway. I would find out soon enough whether it would have mattered much. Although, the mere thought of being in that big ugly institution across town made me feel a bit insecure.

It was near the end of the day—thank the Holy Spirit! After being tortured all day long by all the comments about Cathy Davis and being asked what tribe I was from, it was finally time for seventh period, the last period of the day, with Sister Mary Catherine. I had a few opportunities earlier in the day to work on her assignment, but somehow I kept getting sidetracked. I was glad that none of the other teachers had given me any homework yet. I needed to work my way up to it.

Most of them would soft soap us for the first few days to see how many apples they could collect. It seemed that some of the teachers competed for the affection of the students. Still, I felt that the majority of them just wanted to have a good enough understanding with their pupils. They must have hoped that this would somehow help them to keep us in line throughout the school year.

All through the period, Sister Mary Catherine played blackboard games, and it brought out a little bit of interest from a class that would normally be unenthusiastic from the moment that we took our seats. With white powder from the chalk running down her thick fingers, she wrote down names of important biblical characters or events on the blackboard. Then she pointed to one of us and said, "Let's find out how much time you spent reading the sacred book."

I kept staring at the old clock that was on the wall behind her. I counted down the seconds. One minute to go, I thought. She finally stopped writing on the blackboard. Then she turned toward us. "For those of you that needed some more time, we will go over yesterday's homework at the beginning of class tomorrow."

I just started to grin. I was finally rewarded with one small victory after what seemed like a day of defeats. I made sure that I didn't leave anything on my desk when I walked out of her classroom. I didn't want to ever have to show up that early for school again.

As I left Saint Luke for the day, my mind was cluttered with an array of unusual visions. I thought about everything from making Cathy my squaw—to being scalped by one of the penguins…or even Uncle Joe. There were a few times in the past that they got on my case about the length of my hair. But, then again, if I was the Indian, then I should be doing the scalping.

Then I started to shake my head thinking—enough already! The Indian thing might have just been a family rumor. Even if it was true, I was probably only a small percentage, and somewhere down the line just about everyone else in the country was likely to be part Native American too. They probably should embrace it as well.

With all of the nonsense and confusion that rattled around in my brain as I walked through the schoolyard, it dawned on me that I hadn't seen Ratboy all day. Where was he? I couldn't believe that he would ditch school in the first week. Nobody does that. Was he sick or what? He often looked like there was something wrong with him but he usually made it to school.

In any case it looked like I would be walking home by myself, which always made me feel uncomfortable. Sometimes I would be accosted by one of the public school punks, or by one of the project rejects somewhere between the *safe perimeter* of Saint Luke and the nearly assured safety of my home. Let's just say that it was an uphill climb in more ways than one.

I got to where I was almost halfway home without any trouble. That was the easy part. I still had to make it past not only the hippie house, but I also had to climb the rugged wooden steps that lead to my street—known as the Layers. It was where some of the bad boys would sometimes congregate. They were an eclectic group of mostly teenagers. Some of them were former Saint Luke students. There were others that attended Rockwood, and a few others that were dropouts. They were a diverse group of baby boomers that wanted to rebel with or without a cause. It was kind of a neutral area, but occasionally I would get harassed just for someone's amusement.

Ratboy's older brother used to be one of the area leaders. Whenever he was around, we would get a free pass on our journey without being shaken down. Unfortunately, his brother got sent to Shueville Juvenile Center over the summer for robbing three of his neighbor's houses. Big brother wasn't watching over us anymore. If Ratboy wasn't my walk home companion, then fear was.

As I walked past the hippie house of ill puke, I did a double take. I could have sworn that I saw Ratboy standing right out in the open on the front porch. As I got closer, and the view got more into focus, the Ratboy look-alike proceeded into the doorway. I still wasn't sure if it was him or not, but I didn't dare approach the front door to find out. I just stood frozen in front of the compound-like setting.

As I stood there staring at the porch, one of the long hairs came around from the back of the house and headed my way. I wanted to run, but I couldn't.

He had more tattoos than I could count. They were all over his arms and even on his face. He kept walking toward me.

I tried to shift my feet to run, but…

"Get the hell out of here you little fruit!" He snarled at me while displaying a set of sharp, green teeth.

I still wasn't moving…

Then he started walking closer toward me and continued bellowing, "What do you want, you little shit-ass? Get the hell out of here!"

"No—no—no—nothing….I…uh…was looking for my friend." I finally got my legs to comply with my brain and turned to run. I quickened my pace with every step until I was in a full sprint.

At this speed I separated the distance between myself and Rasputin quickly while hearing him yelling, "Beat it! You don't have any friends here you shit-ass. Don't let me see your scrawny little ass around here again."

My strange and confusing day had become a mesmerizing one. I could feel the rhythm of my footsteps pounding in my head. I remembered hearing a certain term around grownups. The term was *an uncertain world*. I began to understand its meaning.

I didn't know what to do. Part of me wanted to run up to Ratboy's house and tell his mom or dad that he was being held hostage by some aliens, but the biggest part of me wanted to just run home and hide under my bed. In the end all I could do was just keep running. I figured that my feet would point me in the right direction.

I zoomed up the Layers without much trouble, and I made it to my street. Then I foolishly continued my climb toward Ratboy's lair. As I made it near the top, I noticed there were four people glaring at me. One had beady eyes, another was bug-eyed, and the other two had rather unfriendly looks on their faces. The tallest of the four had a scarred face full of puffed out pimples. They were like a younger, less hairy, almost as scary version of the hippies, and I was definitely on their turf. Then I heard, "Get em!"

I went into an abrupt U-turn. I immediately heard their footsteps behind me. I didn't look back . I headed down the dirt path that separated my street from the projects. I hopped over one of the neighbor's fences, and I trespassed across a couple of other properties that were clearly marked *private*. Then I crossed over onto my street, up to my house, through my front door, into my parent's bedroom, and under their bed. Safe at last.

Miraculously, after everything that happened, I was still clutching on to my green book bag that contained my homework. For some insane reason, I started to not only hear, but I also visualized, Gilbert O'Sullivan singing "Alone Again (Naturally)".

The song kept playing over and over in my head. I was in no hurry to move. The combination between the lack of sleep from the night before and an extremely enduring day had exhausted me. I had a hell of a lot to be concerned about. I thought that now I might even need to be chauffeured back and forth to school. That way I could focus more on my Saint Luke issues and less on my traveling obstacles. But, being realistic, I knew that I would have to continue hoofing it to school, and the best possibility I had was to wear a more comfortable pair of shoes. The platforms were stylish and they made me look taller, but that didn't count for shit when mutants were chasing me…or when nuns were lifting me off the ground.

I just continued to lie there for a while. My mind kept going back and forth about…everything. It was way too much for a thirteen year old to have to deal with. I kept thinking about Cathy…and Sister Mary Catherine…and Indians… and hippies, punks, homework, the name of Gilbert's other top forty hit…and… what was the deal with Ratboy?

After about an hour, I crawled out from under the bed without anyone noticing, because I was home alone again. I went upstairs to lie on my own bed to think some more. I remembered being told that my last year at Saint Luke would be challenging, dynamic, and inspirational. This came from Sister Ann Margaret, who spent most of her time sitting on her ass in the school office, or the church, or the convent. I guess she felt that she did her part to get us ready for the world—or at least for Rockwood.

All of the confusion and loneliness that I felt made me want to play with my wiener. I don't know why, but it did. I needed to get a grip on myself, but I just felt like yanking my doodle dandy. It was a neat trick that Ratboy turned me on to when he slept over one night in August.

He said that he did it every day. He said that he even did it in the boy's bathroom at Saint Luke. He told me that he had gotten quite good at it. I noticed that he had several warts on his fingers. Maybe he played with his toad a little too much? I wondered what Sister Ann Margaret would have thought about that.

I had a feeling that I would lie around most of the night and never open my book bag. Of course, that could be highly insulting to Sister Mary Catherine. She already gave me a break, so I didn't want to test her patience. I had enough to worry about. I just needed to get past the first week, and then I would try to figure it all out one step at a time.

Chapter Three

Thank Saint Luke It's Friday

By Friday morning I decided that I would go back to wearing my blue, suede penny loafers—just in case my future required a lot more running. I felt like I had shrunk a couple of inches as I left my house. While walking down the Layers, I noticed Ratboy sitting hunched over at the top of Mannicort Hill. I thought that it would be a good opportunity to try to put an end to the mystery.

When I got to about ten-feet from where he sat, I yelled, "Ratboy! Chuck! Ratboy!" He didn't respond. I walked to the front of him, and I noticed that he was looking down on the ground with his eyes barely open. "Chuck—wake up! Get up! What's the matter with you? Get up!"

He looked up at me with a dazed expression. "Huh?…What? What do you want?" It was almost as if he didn't recognize me.

I started to shake him by the shoulders. "Chuck, you don't look so good. I mean…worse than usual. What's gotten into you?"

He wouldn't say anything. I helped him to his feet—just like I had done many times in the past after he got one of his beatings, but it didn't look like he had gotten beat up this time. He just looked totally out of character—woozy—weird.

We walked down the hill. Well, I walked and he stumbled. He kept looking nervously toward the hippie house as we strolled past it. I thought that he must have had an awful experience inside that damned place. I needed to know more about it before we got to the school.

I kept waiting for him to speak up, to fess up, or maybe he wanted to wait to get inside the confession booth with Father Spencer, which was something that I always had a hard time understanding.

I hated being inside that sin box. I was usually the last one in line. I often considered sneaking out of the church while I waited for my turn, but someone would have probably noticed.

Most of the kids would line up in front of the box like it was a normal procedure—like they were programmed into tiny robots. I just don't understand how reciting three Hail Mary's and four Our Fathers would help us? I heard that Ratboy was terrified the first time he went in. It must have been either being in near total darkness or listening to Father Spencer's deep voice that made him piss his pants on his initial confession. I'm still not sure why, but I know that he did. Ratboy never talked about it.

I could remember when Calvin Gregory was waiting to make his penance on one occasion when we were in sixth grade. He was an outstanding pupil—a clean cut kid. He had bright rosy cheeks and perfect teeth. He reminded me of one of the Osmond brothers—Donny…or maybe their sister, Marie.

I stood behind him, and, just for a laugh, I asked, "What kind of sins do you have to confess, Calvin?"

Looking embarrassed he whispered, "I threw away half of my chipped ham sandwich at lunch yesterday, but I told my mother that I ate the whole thing."

I kept waiting to hear more, but that was all he had. I started to shake my head while saying, "Tsk tsk." Then I said, "You're going to burn in hell, Calvin!"

A concerned look swept across his face.

I went on with, "You better get in there and tell Spencer before it's too late."

He did.

When we got to about a hundred feet past the hippie castle, I decided to interrogate Ratboy. "Chuck, what were you doing in there yesterday?" He continued to ignore me, so I persisted in cross examining him. "I saw you go in yesterday. Don't try to get out of it. You need to tell me now."

He still wasn't saying anything. His face looked awfully pale — sickly — ghostly. He looked like a freaking zombie — day of the living dead, maybe. It was like Ratboy's identity was stolen, and it wasn't really him. I didn't know how he would be able make it through any of his classes. He would probably be sent home early again.

It reminded me of a science fiction program that I watched on television a few weeks earlier. There was an alien spaceship that landed in a suburban neighborhood, and they abducted one of the earthlings. They took the subject to their laboratory and performed a lobotomy. I imagined the hippie palace as being the spaceship. Some of the hippies could have been the aliens, and Ratboy was the unfortunate soul who was abducted.

I got fed up with the whole idea. I grabbed Ratboy by the arm, and yelled about an inch away from his left ear, "Chuck, what the fuck were you doing in the hippie house?"

Looking frightened he yelled back, "My sister goes in there sometimes!"

We continued our dialogue, still almost yelling. "Why does she go in there?"

"She's friends with Matt."

"Who the f… is Matt?"

"He's the one that chased you away yesterday."

I didn't need to know anymore. I knew at that moment that Ratboy would follow the same path as a lot of the other ne'er-do-wells that seemed to congregate just about everywhere between his house and Saint Luke — like his brother — Thaddeus before he got locked up. He was doomed. It was all around him, and the school was no sanctuary either.

I didn't ask him anything else about the hippie episode. We just kept walking together in silence. When we got to the schoolyard, there was a lot of activity going on from one end to the other. I noticed Marty shoving around a couple of seventh graders on one side, while Mike emptied another kid's pocket on the other side.

I looked up to the third floor window, and I saw Uncle Joe in his familiar position—watching over the yard. His focus didn't seem to be on Mike or Marty. In fact, he seemed to be looking over toward us. I stopped walking while Ratboy proceeded ahead, and then there was no doubt in my mind of who was being watched as Uncle Joe's glaring eyeballs moved away from where I stood.

The first morning bell rang, and we all headed inside. I felt pretty good about myself. It was Friday, and suddenly I felt like I would be able to overcome any obstacle that was thrown my way. On top of that, any problem that I had seemed rather small compared to all of Ratboy's frigging issues.

As I walked down the corridor, I noticed that Sister Ann Margaret and Uncle Joe were standing outside of her office. Ratboy was still a few steps ahead of me. When he got to where they were standing, Sister Ann Margaret grabbed him by one of his arms, and Uncle Joe grabbed him by the other. Then, in a semi-evil voice, Uncle Joe said, "We were waiting for you, Mr. Dalton. Where were you yesterday?" Before he got a chance to speak, they dragged him into the office and shut the door.

Only a few seconds went by before I heard the first whack, which was followed by several others. I didn't hear any screaming from him like I had a few other times when some of the other students were being disciplined. Ratboy took it like a man. He was probably used to it by now.

Some of the parents had complained in the past about the staff using excessive corporal punishment. For my final year at Saint Luke, they decided to get signed statements from all of the parents who forbid their child from receiving the paddle. I was one of the first kids to bring the signed statement back to the school.

Most of the other boys, and practically all of the girls, would eventually coax their parents too. Ratboy had no such luck, neither did Marty, and, to my surprise, big shot—Angelo Santino allowed all three of his sons to meet their own fate. I didn't see Ratboy after that. I heard that he was sent home sick for the day.

The rest of the morning I found it hard to concentrate. The classes were so boring, and I kept looking out through the widows and daydreaming about being outside in what appeared to be ideal weather conditions. When I heard the lunch bell ring, I leapt from my seat and ran to the lunchroom. It took me less than five minutes to empty out and wolf down all of the contents that were inside my brown, paper lunch bag. There was a peanut butter and jelly sandwich, Twinkies, and a miniature bag of Fritos—everything that a growing boy needs. My parents allowed me to pack my own lunch.

I also decided to do away with my long standing H.R. Pufnstuf lunchbox for my final year. I had officially become one of the brown baggers—something Ratboy had been since first grade.

When I got out to the yard, I was surprised to see that there were a few others that had beat me to it. Most notably, I saw Cathy Davis who was talking to Sister Theresa—a.k.a. the little Nazi. It was rumored that she kept a hardcover version of Mein Kampf inside of her desk. She was about four-foot-ten, and she always walked with her hands behind her back. She had a very noticeable mustache, zero personality, and a monotone voice that sounded like it came from a cheap AM radio. For some reason I pictured her singing "The Candy Man" in a duet with Sammy Davis Jr.

I finally built up the courage to make my move on Cathy. I just waited for the right moment. It appeared that her conversation with Sister Theresa was winding down as they were moving away from each other. Just then, Cathy looked toward me and winked, or maybe there was just something in her eye. I nervously looked around to determine that if it was a wink, was it meant for me? Nobody else stood near me, so I started to slowly make my advance toward her.

As I got closer to Cathy, I started thinking about what Mike had told me about her letting him use his finger. "Hi, Cathy—nice day, huh?"

"Yea, Tom, how are you doing?"

She kept waiting for me to say something, but I couldn't think of anything interesting to give her. On one side of my brain I could hear Saint Luke saying—be polite, be respectful, be a good Catholic boy. On the other side I could hear Mike Santino saying—finger the slut! My head felt like it might explode, and I felt weak all over. To top it off, my feet felt like they were glued permanently to the ground.

Then, all of a sudden I blurted out, "Cathy, do you think you can lift up your skirt for me, and let me see…uh…?"

Her eyes opened up to full capacity, but she didn't appear to be looking at me. Then I felt someone's hand strenuously grip the back of my right upper arm, and I was quickly spun around. I nearly lost my balance when I saw that it was the little Nazi! She had crept back up on us. She looked really mad. While my body was still spinning toward her, I saw her raise her right hand, and she belted me so hard across the left side of my face that I ended up turning a full three-hundred and sixty degrees back to where I was looking at Cathy again. Sister Theresa immediately grabbed Cathy by the hand and escorted her away.

My head felt like it was fizzing like a recently opened bottle of soda that had been shaken up. I stood there alone…again…naturally. I instinctively looked up at the third floor window and saw Uncle Joe shaking his head. I saw Mike and Tony standing under the basketball hoop. They were laughing hysterically. I stood there thinking about the non-corporal punishment clause. I thought about Mike being full of shit. I thought that I wasn't so thankful to Saint Luke that it was Friday, but I should have listened to his wisdom anyway.

While everyone stared at me, I noticed that Sister Theresa was bringing Cathy inside the school—perhaps to have a little talk with her. Just before they got to the door, Cathy looked back at me and winked again. At that point, I had come to the conclusion that I didn't know anything about life, and I wasn't learning that much inside the classroom either. Maybe I should have told my parents to save their hard earned money and just send me straight to Rockwood.

While I contemplated my present situation, I also felt a stinging sensation on my left cheek. I decided to go inside to the boy's bathroom to look at it. My eyes were getting watery. I made double sure that I correctly walked into the one that was marked BOYS on the door as I thought back to the time when I accidentally went into the one that didn't have urinals inside, and I went into a stall thinking that they were removed for some reason. On that occasion, I sat on the toilet making a mess before I heard unexpected voices.

"Do you think Tommy Richards is cute?" said one voice.

"I think he's kind of weird," said another.

I waited until the voices dissipated. Without making a noisy flush, I ran out of that stinking place and down the hallway. Then I made a U-turn and headed to the door clearly marked BOYS to wash my hands. Since that episode, I always double check. I don't feel too bad about it though, my dad told me that he made a similar mistake once at a local tavern.

When I gazed into the glass, I was horrified to see that Sister Theresa's handprint was quite visible in my reflection. I kept rubbing it, but it wouldn't disappear. I wondered if it would be possible for me to get sent home sick like Ratboy. Then I heard the bell ring to signal the end of the lunch period. So I decided to just tough it out and finish out a not so painless first week of school.

Chapter Four

Well…Maybe Saturday Is Better

When I woke up on Saturday morning, there was only one thing on my mind—BASKETBALL! It was the day of the tryouts. If there was one good thing that Saint Luke was known for it was a legacy of champion hoopsters. What had always impressed me as far back as I could remember was the massive trophy case that was stuffed with shiny metal memories of the athletic prowess of days gone by. There were many photos of the little Catholic boys of yesteryear—the ghosts of Saint Luke. Unfortunately, the two previous seasons, we kind of…uh…stunk—at least compared to some of those great teams. In spite of it we still managed to eke out winning records—though barely.

Coach Morgan decided to get an early start for the season and make us all work our little asses off for a spot on the squad. It was important for me to make the team. It wasn't because I was any good at the game, and it was unlikely that I would see much playing time. However, I still had my reasons.

First and foremost it was the uniform. It was all the achievement that I needed. It meant that I was part of the team, even if I didn't get any floor time. I would let Mike, Marty, and some of the others do the hard work. I would just come along for the ride and hopefully collect a trophy somewhere along the way. I usually got too nervous to want to go in the game anyway, unless we were about thirty points ahead against shitty Saint Mark or Saint John. They were the two teams that we usually beat senseless whenever we played them. We would battle those two Saints at least twice each during the season. If it wasn't for those cake victories, our winning percentage would have dipped well below five-hundred the past two seasons.

On top of that, nobody on the team looked cooler than me. I wore my Chuck Taylors, red sweatbands, headband, and kneepads for all of the games in the previous season. I didn't get to sweat much during any of the games, and all of my apparel would always look brand new because of the minimal need for washing. I was like the team model.

The next best reason was that Cathy Davis was a cheerleader. There would be get-togethers after home games, dark bus rides coming home from away games. And, of course, the cheerleader skirts were even shorter than the ones that the girls wore to class. There wouldn't be much for her to lift up for me to view the goods.

Before I got too far ahead of myself, I needed to make the team first. The coach usually went with only twelve players. There were about twenty kids that showed up. Even though I was a senior, I still only had a slightly better chance of making the team than I did the previous year. There were several seventh graders that had a better shot at making the squad. Even Ratboy decided to try out again. He didn't make the cut last year.

After a grueling four hour workout, Coach Morgan decided to make his choices. The first nine kids were chosen without too much hesitation. One by one they headed up to the locker room in jubilation while the rest of us sat huddled together on the hard wooden gym floor to wait out our fates.

Coach Morgan took his time with the rest of us. He kept walking back and forth while spinning a practice ball on his fat finger. He wanted us to know how important he was and what power he held. He even executed a proud fart as he walked past us. It seemed to blend in well with the stench that came from some of the stinky boys that sat near me.

It wasn't as bad as the bomb that Sister Mary Catherine unloaded on us earlier in the week. It was barely audible, but it was deadly nevertheless. We figured that she shit herself when she exclaimed, "Oh dear!" Then I was certain that she crapped in her undergarments when she said, "I'll be right back class," and she abruptly left the classroom to go compose herself. It wasn't the first time that she broke wind in front of us. She needed to seriously consider changing her dietary habits.

As Morgan's fart faded, we all just sat there as our bodies gradually dried out from all of the dripping sweat. We remained totally silent as he was about to make his final selections. I kept thinking that I didn't want to go home and tell the folks that I wasn't able to make the team.

When I got to the point that I couldn't handle much more suspense nor tolerate the body odor that reeked from Ratboy and a few others, the Coach looked at me and pointed. "Okay, Richards—you made it. You can go upstairs."

Both of my feet had fallen asleep, but I quickly lifted myself off of the floor anyway. Feeling victorious I happily limped my way up to the locker room, but I knew that another fate was still waiting for me. It didn't matter that I was a senior, or that I was on the team the previous year. The bullies felt that they needed to initiate the rest of us any way that they saw fit. I tried to prepare my state of mind as I walked up the steps.

As soon as I opened the locker room door, there was Mike and Marty—who were destined to be the co-captains—whipping everyone with towels. When they saw me, they said—almost simultaneously, "Did you make it, Tom?"

"I sure did."

Then I covered up my face and walked through the thrashing. I was still somewhat relieved knowing that they would expend most of their energy on the seventh graders or anyone that they felt needed a good dose of pain. I knew that I would get off fairly easy compared to what some of the others would have to go through.

I looked around the locker room to assess the damage. One of the tortured boys had a streak a blood trailing down his leg. Another kid was lying on the ground with his hands over his jock strap. He looked like he was trying to hold his balls in place. I couldn't help to think that Mike and Marty were still conserving a good bit of energy for the last two winners…or losers?

The last ten kids that were waiting in the gym were comprised of poor Ratboy and a few other uncoordinated non-hopefuls. I instinctively took a seat in the corner where I had a full view of the doorway. I guess that I always had a curiosity for some of society's violent tendencies…as long as someone else was the victim.

A few minutes later I could hear lucky number eleven hustling up the stairway. M and M were able to have sufficient time to rest before pouncing on their next prey. The door opened wide, and I saw that it was Stanley Howard — a seventh grader who wore thick glasses and had a big smile on his face. In a matter of seconds, both the smile and the glasses had disappeared, and several tears had taken their place.

It was bad enough that I had to turn away for a moment. I sat there wondering who the sadist was that thought up this kind of torture as a grand way to welcome an unsuspecting youth into a brotherhood of sorts. I wondered if Coach Morgan knew about it, or even Uncle Joe for that matter. He seemed to always be lurking around the gym for some reason.

Perhaps the two of them played here at one time, and maybe they were the ones that originated the brutal hazing. Both of them seemed to have the personality for it, and so did some of the nuns for that matter. I remembered seeing Sister Mary Catherine shooting a few balls in the schoolyard during lunch period. I wondered what Saint Luke was like in real life. I wondered what some of the old time players in the photos that were tucked inside the trophy case would have thought about the whole idea.

As I continued to ponder, I heard the final selection making his way up the steps. I had a funny feeling about who it would be. When I saw the door begin to open, I turned toward my locker again and I started to get changed. I listened to the towels whipping in the air, and M & M shouting assorted expletives. I' m sure it was brutal. I should know because I was the twelfth pick the previous year. At least, I was well liked by some of the executioners.

As usual I avoided taking a shower. It was still too embarrassing for me to share one large shower with several other boys, especially since I knew that M&M would take control of it too. I didn't want anyone to see my puny, hairless penis. It was also getting stiff fairly often—ever since Ratboy taught me how to jerk-off. It especially got lively whenever I thought about Cathy. I didn't want any of the guys to think that I was a homo if it started to grow at the wrong moment.

While I packed up my gym bag, I noticed that M&M—long with a few other kids were playing shower hockey with a large bar of Ivory soap. From the corner of my left eye, I saw Ratboy stripping down, and then he foolishly headed into the steam. I didn't want to stick around for what was coming next.

I hurried for the exit, but before I could get there, I heard horrible laughter—along with someone yelling repeatedly, "Elephant trunk! Elephant trunk! Elephant trunk!" I immediately thought back to our jerk off session, and I remembered Chuck showing me that he wasn't circumcised. I even allowed him to touch the head of my penis because I felt sorry for him. I left the gym thinking that I might not be afraid to take a shower next time. If Ratboy could do it—then so could I…maybe?

I walked home thinking that there was almost nothing that I enjoyed about the tryouts. I was tired, sore, embarrassed, smelly, and even a bit angry. I knew that I had no chance of being a star, and I would get plenty of rest during the games. It was what the faces in the trophy case told me to do. It's what Saint Luke wanted for me. It was my destiny…I thought.

I mostly sat around for the remainder of the weekend. I felt a bit disappointed. So what, I made it to eighth grade—I made the team—rah! Rah! Did the good outweigh the bad? Was Saint Luke really the great institution that we were told it was from the time we were preschoolers? Was it the best that our hardworking parents' dollars could buy? Would the memories be golden and the bonds inseparable? I was told that only God knew the answers, which was another piece of divine wisdom that was handed down to me from generations past, but was it fact or fiction?

The not so funny thing was that I could count on two fingers how many people at the school that I really cared for, or about. It certainly wasn't Mike or Marty, or Coach Morgan, or any of the nuns, or even Uncle Joe. Nope. It was the two people that were mostly disliked by everyone else — the slut and the kid that everyone wanted to beat up. It was like my grandfather would say — "that's life…who can explain it?"

Chapter Five
The Church Is the Place to Be

As September rolled along, familiar patterns had developed everywhere. I saw Ratboy going into the hippie house on several occasions, and he continued to get smacked around by just about everyone—except me. Even though I'd been tempted on more than one occasion to do my part to keep him in line, I never did. His personality kept changing. He seemed to be getting a lot lazier. It was like he was sedated or under some type of hypnosis. I decided that I would make it a priority to keep an eye on him, as did Uncle Joe and Sister Ann Margaret.

Mike and Marty continued to rule the schoolyard. I don't think that they even liked each other, but they seemed to form a truce since their much talked about—nearly legendary brawl. I guess they figured that it would be a lot easier to shove the weaker kids around than it would be to combat each other.

Mike also seemed to be bringing his brother Tony, a seventh grader up through the ranks. Occasionally, even his youngest brother, Angelo Junior would be in the mix. He was only in fifth grade, which meant that the high flying Santino brothers would be able to rule the yard for a few more years. All three of them always seemed to have a load of coins jingling in their pockets.

Uncle Joe kept a careful eye on the brothers, but he was even more careful not to pounce. Even though the school never got a single don't beat my kids letter from Don Angelo Senior, Uncle Joe didn't want to risk an ugly visit from him either. I was already bored with the entire situation, but things were about to change for me forever.

On a rainy, late September afternoon, Cathy Davis waited outside the school underneath a large red and yellow umbrella. I didn't know if she was waiting for a ride or…somebody?

"Hi, Cathy, are you waiting for someone?"

"Yea, I'm waiting for Tom."

I pondered for a moment trying to decipher who she was referring to. When I got to the point that I looked about as confused as humanly possible, she moved closer to me and told me that there was plenty of room for both of us under the umbrella. At that point, I couldn't think of another Tom that went to Saint Luke—with the exception of Calvin Gregory's little brother, but I think he was only in third…or fourth grade. When she grabbed my hand, I was almost sure that I was the Tom that she was waiting for.

She pulled me along with her as if she was on some kind of mission, but probably not a religious one. My face was flush with embarrassment. I offered no resistance at all. We walked to the end of the yard, down the side of the school, and then toward the church. I wasn't sure where she was taking me. I was happy and a little scared at the same time.

The rain started splashing down a lot heavier, and we took a quick detour at the side of the church. We walked down a small flight of steps and underneath an awning. She shook the rain out of her umbrella while I stared at an old wooden door that had a metal cross embossed into it. It stood there like a reminder of all the lessons I had been taught by the penguins over the years.

Feeling extremely nervous, I tried twisting the knob, and then she whispered, "It won't open. They only use this entrance when they are having mass on Sunday."

I wondered why she knew about it, but only for a brief moment. I definitely knew which one of us was the teacher, and who was the student. Cathy was probably the most mature thirteen-year old that I would ever know. Some people might have had alternate descriptions for her. For the time being, I was her little puppet. She knew that she could run the show. I was rather passive. She was the one in charge. We both knew our places well enough.

She had certainly met my fancy, but at the same time, I figured her to be a bit of a tomboy…or at least I used to think that way. I was intrigued by the idea that, if I didn't comply with her wishes, she might have to gently beat the crap out of me. That could have been embarrassing for me if it got around the school, so there was only one way for me to go. Before I knew it, her face was about an inch away from mine.

"Do you know how to French kiss?"

"Uh…yea…of course…I…uh…" I lied.

I was still struggling to get words out when she shoved her tongue in my mouth. I was a little shocked at first. It felt like it made it halfway down my throat. It was weird, but it was still better than anything I was being taught in any of my classes at Saint Luke. I wasn't sure what to do, or how long it was supposed to last. I certainly wasn't ready for it, because there was way too much saliva building up in my mouth. A little had already dribbled on my chin. I began to choke. I had to end it quickly. I turned away from her to wipe my chin, and I shamefully spit a mixture of our saliva onto the holy ground.

She looked at me somewhat disappointed. "What's the matter? Don't you like it?" She rolled her tongue across her lips.

"No…I…uh.…"

Before I could offer an explanation, her slippery tongue had made its way back. This time I was ready, and I decided to see what my tongue was capable of doing. We started to go into a tongue roll, and it was strangely wonderful. I still felt awkward, but this time I was content to be inside of her mouth.

After a long, calorie-sin burning session, she pulled out her tongue and dragged it across my face and into my ear. It nearly made me jump out of my shoes. I felt myself shiver when she said softly, "I thought you were going to lift up my skirt, Tom. What are you waiting for?"

For once, everything seemed to be working for me. The tuition had partially paid off, and there weren't any nuns in sight to slap me around. I sat her down on the step, and I knew that the time was right for me to make a move—a big step at the bottom of the small steps.

I was so excited that I couldn't control my heavy breathing. She just sat there totally relaxed like she knew what it was all about. I lifted up her skirt, and she spread her legs w-i-d-e. I started rubbing my hand over her underpants. It felt warm, and to my surprise—a little bit wet! I hoped that she wasn't sick or something.

She decided not to wait for me to pull her underwear down. It was the strangest thing. She was like a woman that was waiting to be pleasured, and I was like a little boy that was toying around with silly putty. I thought she was a few months older than me, but maybe she was even older than that. I noticed that there was a small crevice that my finger slipped into very nicely. I decided to experiment with two fingers, and I wondered if three would be a crowd. I didn't get any complaints from her, just a little bit of oohing and aahing.

While I continued my three finger dance, she crept her body forward and grabbed me from behind the neck. She started to pull my head toward her, and I thought that perhaps she wanted to visit France again. Instead, she guided my head in the direction of where her underpants used to be, and I determined that she had a whole different country in mind somewhere down under.

I didn't know what she expected, and I found it to be both exhilarating and frightening. She didn't stop being forceful until my lips met her…well, other lips. It tasted funny, and it smelled even funnier, but I wasn't laughing. I just rested there and continued my heavy breathing. Just to make the most out of the experience, I started rubbing my cheeks back and forth over her little bit of peach fuzz. It tickled both of us, and she let out a giggle. I started thinking that it was probably the kind of thing that adults did when they were alone late at night.

All of a sudden, it got too quiet. I looked up, and I noticed that the rain had stopped. Cathy pulled up her underwear, and then she reached into her book bag for a pack of Salem cigarettes. She also had one of those fancy, Bic lighters that shot up like a torch. She reminded me of some old floozy that I remembered seeing in a movie when I was up unusually late one night. I also noticed that she wore a little bit of lipstick and makeup that was smudged over a few places on her face, and on my shirt collar too. I tried to be a man inside of a boy's body…hell, a boy's mind for that matter. I wondered why my penis didn't get hard the whole time, when there had been several occasions in the past where just the mere thought of being alone with her had done the dick trick.

As she sat there puffing away, she looked at me. "Do you know how to French, Tom?"

I sat there thinking…didn't we cover this already? Then she showed me a neat inhaling trick while adjusting her tongue and lower lip in a different way. She seemed to be a well versed, and well-traveled woman, and I was still a little boy that rarely ventured beyond the small area between my home and Saint Luke.

She passed the cigarette to me. There was a tiny bit of lipstick on the filter too. "Go ahead and take a drag. Go ahead," she urged.

I tried it only once before with Ratboy, and I hated it then. Of course, just like that occasion, I pretended that I was hip to the idea, and just like that time I took too big of a drag. I quickly remembered why I hated it so much. It certainly didn't help my standing in regards to acting like a man to be choking like a fool in front of Cathy. On the other hand, I already scored a basket. I made my free throw. I took another small puff, and then I gladly handed it back to her.

A narrow sliver of sunshine had made its way through a small slit in the front of the awning that was above us. I followed its path through Cathy's golden hair all the way down to where the light rested on the metal cross. When I looked at it, I was nearly blinded. I knew at that moment that I had certainly sinned. I comforted myself by thinking that it was all Cathy's fault, and that she would have to be the one to repent to the almighty being—not me. I was coaxed into the sinful situation.

She had a casual look on her face though. I didn't think that she was worried about a damn thing. I didn't know if that was good or bad. I didn't know anything. Actually, I did know one thing. I knew that I sure as hell didn't want to go into the box to confess it all to Father Spencer. He would have probably told me to recite one million Our Fathers, two million Hail Mary's, and then had me walk on hot coals. Maybe he would have expelled me from the church and school for life. Either way, I only felt mildly guilty, and I finally felt my penis getting a bit larger.

Cathy butted out her smoke on the step. "Do you want to walk me home now, Tom?" As she waited for an answer, she added, "I don't live very far from here."

I knew that she only lived a few blocks away. So I guess that it wouldn't be too much trouble as long as she didn't ask me to hold her hand or would want me to kiss her in public. "Yea—sure—okay. Let's go."

We walked back up the steps, and there still wasn't anyone around. We did it, and I got away with it! Although, I thought that we may have broken one of the Holy Commandments, but we were just kids, so it might not have counted against us yet. We probably didn't qualify for adultery. I wondered if there was a younger version—childtery, or something? Then I remembered that you had to belong to someone else first, or covet someone or something to break that commandment anyway. I wasn't sure how it all worked. We may not have even qualified as official sinners yet.

I started feeling good about the whole affair, and my little guy felt like it was finally stretched out to its maximum length. I don't think that Cathy even noticed it. That was one big advantage I had because my little guy was truly a little guy. I was able to get away with it in Science class one time when Sister Theresa asked me to come up to the chalkboard to answer a question regarding different types of wood. It could have been a painful experience for someone more endowed. It was almost a breeze for me—almost.

As we started walking toward her house, it started drizzling again. Usually I hated to get wet, but I didn't seem to mind on this day. It felt enchanting. I felt like singing in the rain. Cathy was probably feeling it too because she didn't even bother to open the umbrella. She didn't ask me to hold her hand either. To my surprise, she asked, "Are you going to get me a ring, Tom?"

"You mean…like from a cracker jack box or something?"

"No, silly boy—a real ring—you know."

"Uh…is this your house here, Cathy?"

"Yea, did you want to come inside for a while?"

I wanted to get the hell out of there, but she was still waiting for an answer to either the…are you going to get me a ring question, or the…did you want to come inside for a while question. I just stood there frozen in time with the rhythm of the raindrops tapping on my skull. I wanted to turn my body toward the direction homeward, but my feet and legs weren't quite ready to cooperate yet.

Just then I noticed her big brother looking out the window. He was in eighth grade at Saint Luke when I was in sixth, and he always looked at me like I was some kind of sissy boy. I wasn't sure if I wanted to stay out in the rain or take a chance inside for possible pain. I didn't like any of my options, and Cathy looked bored. Suddenly, she grabbed my face and kissed me on the lips. "See you tomorrow, Tommy boy." She seemed like she tried to make a point emphasizing the word boy.

That wasn't too bad though, I thought as I started walking away. I hoped that she was only kidding about the asking for a ring business. I was sure that I would find out soon enough. Either way I felt that it was a great achievement for me. I was torn between keeping my afternoon of lust to myself or blabbing it to some of the guys along with heavy exaggerations.

By the time I made it home, I decided to wait and see how Cathy would handle it. I would let her control the game ball for the time being. If it was in my hands, there was too great of a chance that I would end up double dribbling…or fouling out.

Chapter Six

The Church Is the Place to Be—Part Two

Nearly a week had passed since my *wild sex romp* at the side of the church with Cathy. To my surprise, whenever I saw her, she never mentioned anything about it to me. I was happy that she stopped asking me about a ring or going steady. I was also glad that I didn't have to hear about our lustful adventure from anyone else, which meant that both of us decided to stay hush-hush. I was relieved but at the same time—mildly disappointed. I guess that I really wanted more, and I hoped that there would be another opportunity for me to visit the old church again.

It was early October, and the cool autumn breeze was blowing through the big yard. Mike, Ratboy, and I were standing underneath an old rusty hoop and, rather lazily, tossing the ball against the backboard. I think that we were all wondering if we could get into any mischief before the end of the lunch period.

Mike's brother Tony, who was the school's merry prankster, and an experienced altar boy, came running toward us. "Hey, do you guys want to sneak into the church with me right now?"

Mike bounced the ball off of Tony's forehead and said with an annoyed expression, "What for dickhead?"

"You'll see, come on, follow me," Tony said temptingly as he started walking toward the sacred place.

I was certainly interested, and I thought that Ratboy might be too. I asked Tony, "Can Chuck come along with us?"

I had to ask him because Ratboy wasn't always automatically included in all of the activities. Some of the kids didn't want to be seen with him. There was once a rumor going around that Ratboy carried fleas, lice, or some other type of bug on his body.

"I don't care. Come on—let's go. We don't have a lot of time," Tony urged.

Even Mike was intrigued as he dropped the ball on the ground and kicked it toward a group of sixth graders, and called out, "Wait up for me, guys!"

We only had about fifteen minutes to kill, so we all started jogging down along the side of the school. Tony made a right turn toward the back of the building. He appeared to be taking a shortcut down a little dirt path. We followed him through some thick bushes and onto a brick walkway. He looked back and whispered, "This is the priest's entrance." Then he pulled an old, crusty looking key out of his pocket and turned it in the lock of a thick wooden door until we heard a click.

Tony looked like he knew exactly what he was doing when he walked inside. The rest of us hesitated as we stood outside of the large, intimidating entrance. A statue of Saint Luke gazed at us suspiciously. We looked around nervously before we proceeded one by one. It felt a bit like Mission Impossible. I was fascinated by the possibilities.

I was the last to go in. I had already taken a big risk in keeping within the good graces of the church the previous week with Cathy. I knew that I was pushing my luck, but it was too late to back out. Besides, I wanted to see every sleight of hand that Tony was prepared to show us.

Tony had a hell of a lot of balls for a seventh grader. When I walked in, he was already rummaging through the cabinets. He pulled out a small cardboard box. "Look at this, guys. Come here—look!"

We gathered around him as he pulled out a plastic bag from inside the box. It was filled with thousands of little Communion hosts. Tony grabbed a few and said, "Try them—they're pretty good."

While Tony chomped away, Ratboy and I looked at each other not being sure if we wanted to partake. "Don't worry about it, guys. They're not even blessed yet," Tony promised.

I stuffed four of the virgin wafers into my mouth and they quickly stuck to my roof. "Man, these things are dry!" I started to cough while Tony and Ratboy kept munching away.

Just then Mike tapped me on the shoulder. I turned around and saw that he was holding a bottle with a label that read Altar Wine. I kept trying to loosen the stuck on hosts with my tongue while Mike twisted off the bottle cap. He took the first swig, and I couldn't resist with the second one. I stared at the bottle and noticed the small print that read 2% Alcohol. I didn't know if that amount was a lot or a little, but I did know that we came to the right place to be sinners.

Tony, Mike, and I kept passing the bottle around until it was about two thirds empty. Ratboy was still busy stuffing his face with the little wafers, and then stuffing his pockets with a few miniature candles that he found inside of another box.

"Tony, what if Father Spencer comes in here?" I asked.

"Don't worry about it. I work here. Come check this out!"

He walked out onto the altar like a seasoned performer entering the stage to do a sound check, grabbed a microphone, and turned on the switch. "Testing—testing—1—2—3—testing." His amplified voice seemed to be echoing off the stained glass windows and bouncing off of the pews. The church had somehow transformed into Madison Square Garden.

Mike and I noticed that there were two more microphones. Then we lunged for them while giggling with excitement. We started by yelling out a few fitting expletives and seeing who could yell the loudest. "Jesus Christ! Holy shit!" Then, the rock opera ensued.

Tony belted out the first notes to Smoke on the Water. Mike and I offered vocal assistance with some of the lyrics. Then, all three of us tried to harmonize the chorus.

Three make believe guitars were blazing along with me and Mike mouthing the song's riff. Tony pretended that he was Ritchie Blackmore smashing his guitar on stage. It was shear artistic beauty. As much fun as the three of us were having, Ratboy had his own little scheme in the works. He was working his hand down into one of the poor boxes and attempting to make a sizeable withdraw.

We were so worked up into a frenzy that we weren't even thinking about the possible consequences of our mission. We had no idea if lunch time was over yet, nor did we care. We also didn't realize that the Minister of Darkness—Father Spencer was hiding in the shadows, just behind a white pillar next to the confession box until we heard his deep, dark, evil voice yell, "What are you doing in here?" He wasn't looking at us three rock gods. No, he had his eyes firmly set on Ratboy. "I said, what are you doing in here, boy?"

Ratboy started rushing toward the back entrance while yelling, "Nothing. I came in here to pray!"

Pastor Spencer wasn't buying it. He started down the aisle after the fleeing robber while yelling, "Stop! Wait! Hold it—you! Come back here this minute!"

The three of us swiftly left the altar and headed back in the direction that we had entered, but before we made it outside, we noticed through the window that Spencer's left hand man, Father Murphy, was heading toward us. We were like three little church mice looking for an escape route. The problem was that we hadn't been as quiet as church mice.

We ran back to the altar, and then we headed toward the side entrance. Tony mumbled, "Christ, I'm supposed to get five bucks for working a wedding this weekend."

Mike responded with, "I thought you said that you got ten bucks for weddings."

Tony corrected him with, "No, that's for funerals."

As we made it to the side entrance, I thought—that's a pretty nice racket. I had no idea that the altar boys were paid anything—let alone that much loot. Tony turned the lock, and we were finally back outside. Another reminder of my continuous sinning lay on the ground outside the door—Cathy's Bic lighter. She must have dropped it when we were here recently, but I didn't have time to pick it up. Perhaps it was an omen of sorts. Could a simple door to the side entrance of a church have more meaning for me? Was it a reminder of Cathy, or sex, or sin, or heaven...or hell?

We sped up to the top of the steps. Tony and Mike kept running toward the schoolyard. I was curious as to what had happened to Ratboy. I cautiously walked toward the back entrance of the church and peeked around the corner. I was able to hear voices coming from the top of the steps. Then, I witnessed one of the most unusual sights that could possibly be seen in such a setting. Was it a bird or a plane? No…it was Super Ratboy flying off the steps. Except, the awkward way that his body was twisted about, and the velocity that he was traveling, gave me the impression that he was thrown from the top of the steps. Who would do such a thing? It looked painfully obvious.

I didn't wait for him to make a full landing. I decided that I should head back to the school. When I got back to the yard, I saw that it was deserted. I hurried inside and sprinted down the hallway. Mrs. Bun, one of the few non-nun female teachers in the school, was still standing outside her classroom door. I guess that she wanted to know why there were still two empty seats in the room several minutes after the late bell rang.

As I approached Mrs. Bun, she had her arms folded while tapping her right foot on the linoleum. In a snobbish way, she questioned, "You decided to grace us with your presence have you, Mr. Richards?"

"Yes, Mrs. Bun...I...uh...thought...uh...."

"And, where is your partner in crime—Mr. Dalton—pray tell?"

I wondered if she knew more than she let on. She used the words crime and pray in the same sentence, which pretty much summed up Ratboy's whole episode. He pretended that he went into the church to pray while committing a serious crime. It was too coincidental. I wondered how she could know anything already. Did she have ESP?

"Uh…I haven't seen him, Mrs. Bun. I don't know where he is."

She just pointed toward my desk. "Take your seat—you dirty bum." She always made us boys feel like second *class* citizens. She was always neatly dressed and well spoken. I think she made an impression on some of the girls, but they probably just pretended to look up to her.

Some of my classmates started to giggle, and I heard someone whisper, "Richards is Bun's bum."

I just sat at my desk like a nervous little sinner while only half-listening to Mrs. Bun's daily lecture. Ratboy never showed up, and I had a pretty good feeling that I wouldn't get off so easy either. I could barely believe that Father Spencer would be angry enough to throw him down the steps. Maybe, Ratboy tried to jump and got tripped up somehow. I thought about it briefly, and then I whispered to myself, "No—no, he was definitely thrown all the way down."

About halfway through the class, I heard a tap on the door. Mrs. Bun said, "Excuse me for a moment, class."

She opened the door and greeted Sister Ann Margaret. They stepped into the hallway and spoke quietly for about a minute or two while occasionally throwing a glance toward me. It felt like everyone in the classroom, and in the heavens above, was staring at me.

Then, Sister Ann Margaret stepped inside the room and requested, "Mr. Richards, can you come with me please?"

As I stood up, I heard several of my classmates whispering. Mrs. Bun stood there shaking her head while adjusting her oversized glasses. Sister Ann Margaret stood in the hallway while waving me toward her. As I began walking out of the room, I heard, "Oooooooh" coming from a few childish voices behind me.

When I got out to the hallway, Sister Ann Margaret rested her hand on my shoulder. "Father Spencer wants to have a word with you. He's waiting for you in my office."

I was tempted to mention to her that he wasn't permitted to lay a hand on me, but I just kept quiet instead. Besides, the no beating document didn't keep Sister Theresa from slapping my face off when she heard me ask Cathy to lift up her skirt in the schoolyard. It was a few weeks since that incident occurred, and I could still see part of her handprint on my face whenever I looked in the mirror. I never complained about it. I never mentioned it to my parents either. What could I have said to them? How would I have explained it all?

We made it to the principal's office, and Sister Ann Margaret directed me to the back room. It was dimly lit and had a musty smell. Pastor Spencer sat at an old, withered desk while writing intensely into his tablet. Perhaps the mustiness came from him. He didn't seem to notice me right away. I just stood there quietly and motionless. Then he looked up for a second. "Close the door and have a seat, Mr. Richards."

He continued writing quite vigorously for several minutes while I just sat there waiting. When I started to look around the room, I heard the tip of his pencil break. I looked back at him as he dropped the pencil on to the tablet and sighed. He still wasn't looking at me, but he began to speak anyway. "Since you like to spend so much time around the church, I'm sure you wouldn't mind volunteering for altar boy service, right?"

I certainly didn't see that one coming. I hated the thought of it. I wondered if he knew anything about the incident I had with Cathy. While he waited for an answer, I started thinking about that ridiculous robe I would have to wear. I thought that maybe I would have traded that kind of embarrassment for an immediate and firm beating. Then I thought about the cash that Tony claimed to make, but Father did say — "volunteer". What a gyp!

He finally looked up at me. "Uh...well...uh...." His expression became grimmer. I took a deep swallow. "Yes, Father Spencer, I can...uh...volunteer."

"That's good...that's good...Mr. Dalton also volunteered. I will see both of you this Saturday morning at nine o'clock sharp for training at your favorite place." Then he looked down again and just waived me off.

As I was leaving the room, I couldn't resist asking. "Is Chuck in school, Father?"

Once again he wouldn't look up. "No…Mr. Dalton had an unfortunate accident. He was sent home for the day."

I left there thinking about how many times I could remember Ratboy being sent home for having accidents, being sick, or for disciplinary matters. Maybe the reason he was held back a year…or two was because he hadn't been able to put in his time.

He had to do two weeks of summer school after we completed seventh grade, but he told me that he missed half of those days also.

I walked out of the principal's office wondering why only Ratboy and I had to volunteer, and not Mike. Then I thought that Spencer already had Tony, and one Santino brother was probably enough. It was like what Sister Mary Catherine told us about the old days when one child from each devoted Catholic family would become a nun or a priest. They tried to keep that foolish tradition going with the altar boys, I guess. Of course, few of us had that kind of devotion.

I had one other dilemma though. Our first basketball game was on Saturday afternoon. So I hoped that the altar boy training would be short. I knew that I would be awfully miserable sitting in the church all day smelling candle wax and old wooden pews. I would much prefer being in the gym or even the locker room smelling sweat.

I finally finished my last class for what seemed like a longer than usual day at Saint Luke. As I walked down the hallway toward the exit, I could hear the rain coming down. I remembered once hearing the term déjà vu from one of the teachers. I didn't understand its full meaning until I saw Cathy once again standing under an umbrella outside of the entrance. Although, this time she had a green umbrella that happened to match her spike heeled shoes. She was becoming more fashionable. I couldn't decide if she more resembled a movie actress or a street hooker. Either way the rosy lipstick made her most appealing.

As I approached her, I didn't have to ask her who she was waiting for like I did the previous time. When you know—you just know. I thought that I would have fun with her when I asked, "So…what are you up to, Cathy?"

"What do you think, Tom? I thought that you might want to go for a walk with me."

"Well…I'm kind of busy…but…."

I didn't want to say yes. I didn't want to say no. But, once again, she grabbed my hand and led the way. She was quite an aggressive girl, and I think that I liked it. Actually, I know that I liked it. We seemed to be retracing our previous steps from a week earlier, and heading for that familiar place.

When we were near our infamous locale, she looked at me and said, "There's no one home at my house if you would like to…you know."

She was full of surprises, and even though it pleased me all over, I still started to shiver a little. I'm sure it was partly because of some nervous energy that was building up inside me, and partly because of the cold wind that the storm had brought with it. She picked up on it and she instinctively started to comfort me by rubbing my shoulder with her free hand. That was something that I had only experienced before with my mom. Once again, I felt as if I was with a mature woman.

As my shaking subsided, the reality of the situation started to kick in, and I asked, "Isn't your mom at home right now?"

"No, she's working. She won't be home until at least five o'clock."

"How about your dad then?"

"No, he's dead."

"Oh…I'm sorry…to…uh…. What about your brother?"

"He won't be home until later either."

I ran out of good questions. "Do you have any Nestles Quick at your house?"

"I don't know, but we won't have time for that anyway."

"Oh…I…uh…." I wasn't sure what she meant by that.

I felt so passive with her that I was worried that I would pee my pants. I wanted her to take control of me. Once again, I wanted to be her little puppet. I think that she knew this and she would most likely take charge of the whole situation. Just like before, I was both excited and frightened at the same time.

As we were walking together, I kept fantasizing about all of the possibilities. I imagined nakedness…sucker bites…French kisses…rubbing her little fuzzy…getting the crap beat out of me…Nestles Quick…her family showing up and seeing me naked…her dead father's rotten corpse staring at me. She was still holding my extremely sweaty palm during my entire fantasy trip.

We finally arrived at her front gate. I noticed some movement at the same window that her brother was looking out the last time I was here. "Cathy, I thought you said there wasn't anyone home."

"There isn't anyone home." She saw that I was hesitating. Then she grabbed my hand. "Come on in."

When Cathy opened her front door, a muscular bulldog was there to greet us. She immediately grabbed hold of him. I thought it might be a good time to try to build up my courage. As soon as I walked into the house I tried to pet him, but Cathy lost control of her guard dog, and he lunged at me. "Ah! Ah!" I started to scream as I fell to the ground. "Ah! Ah!" I tried to cover myself up. The beast never bit me. He just stood on top of me and barked. I noticed that his collar had several little metal crosses engraved into it.

Like a coward, I continued yelling, "Ahh! Ahh! Get him off of me, please!"

Cathy yelled, "Heel, Jesus! Heel, boy!" Then she started beating him with a rolled up Catholic newspaper. The dog let out a yelp when Cathy accidentally drove her spike heel into one of his paws.

Cathy did her best to restrain the beast, and she eventually took Jesus into the cellar to crucify him further. Jesus kept up a steady stream of loud barking to let me know that it was his turf and she was his to protect, but Cathy let the beast know that it was her turf, and I was hers to protect.

She took her time with Jesus in the basement. I was still lying on the floor with my right ear pressed to it. Over the dog's loud barks, I could have sworn that I heard the snapping of a bullwhip.

Then shortly after that, it sounded like the pounding of a hammer. I thought about crucifixion. I also envisioned my grandfather cracking his old beagle Ralph in the skull with a ballpeen hammer when one of them went mad.

Jesus finally decided to calm down.

I got up off the ground and started walking around her house. Everywhere I looked there were crosses, images of Christ, and long, white candles. I soon realized that I was in a hypocrite's house of sin. I remembered her mom being very involved with the church—except for Friday and Saturday nights when she was supposedly drinking and whoring it up at the Shamrock Inn.

My grandfather once told me that the God fearing types were usually the biggest sinners. They would go to the church to bury their shame. He would never go there, and even my parents rarely would. I just wanted to be mischievous. Cathy was a born sinner. She knew it, and she loved it. I hoped that she didn't want to make me her personal sacrifice…then again.…

When Cathy came up from the basement, she immediately invited me up to her bedroom on the second floor. Her room was also loaded with religious paraphernalia. "Would you like to see some of my pictures, Tom? I got lots and lots of them."

"Sure, okay."

"I put it together all by myself."

I didn't care. But out of courtesy, I responded with, "Okay, cool…let's see it!"

She pulled out a huge makeshift book that was tucked under her bed. "I spent a lot of time putting all of these collages together." She gave me the history of each one.

I tried to be patient, but after about ten minutes the photos were boring the shit out of me. I wanted action. I turned away for a moment, and then I heard a loud thud! I quickly turned back toward her, and I noticed that she dropped the massive book on the floor. Without saying a word, she forcefully pinned me down on the bed. She started licking my lips. Then she started biting my lips. What a strange feeling it was. Was I supposed to be some kind of gourmet meal for her? I wondered what far off land she originated from. Where did they grow her? Was she from a different world altogether?

One thing for certain was that all of the nibbling and sucking that she was doing on my face, lips, neck, and ears would certainly leave some marks, but I wasn't overly concerned about it at the moment. I was however…a bit overwhelmed. It was kind of freaky.

I didn't know what to expect next. I couldn't even say that I enjoyed it all that much. I just lay there and passed the time away. I noticed a small clock that sat on top of her huge dresser, but the second hand didn't seem to be moving. The time was probably off too. Maybe time didn't matter when you were in her bedroom of sin.

When she eventually finished her feeding frenzy, she loosened her grip on me and asked, "Do you want to watch television? I think The Electric Company is on right now."

What an odd change of direction. I was amazed that she went from nearly devouring me to wanting to watch some educational program. I didn't care to watch such a juvenile show, and I was surprised that she did. I just shook my head. "No, I got to go home and…find where I lost my baseball glove." I considered it to be a good escape clause.

"What? What are you talking about? Baseball glove? Are you kidding me, Tom?"

"Nothing…do you want to do…anything else?"

"She gave me a sly grin, and asked, "Do you want to smoke something good?"

"No…I…uh…do you have any Nestles…uh…?"

"I don't mean cigarettes. I mean…something else that I found in my brother's drawer when I was in his room yesterday."

I started imagining her brother beating me up again, and I started rubbing my right ear because it felt uncomfortable from her biting it for so long. "No, I gotta go. I'll see you at school tomorrow, okay?"

I walked quickly out of her room, and I leaped down the stairwell. I didn't want to press my luck. I certainly didn't want her to start biting me again. I didn't want the dog or any of her family members—living or dead to bite me either. I decided to go home to get a bite to eat instead. I obviously had biting on my mind, and unfortunately, all over my face and neck. I thought that maybe I shouldn't have taken that walk after all.

After my two encounters with Cathy, I couldn't decide if I wanted to remain a boy for a while, become a man really quick, or maybe a little of both. It was certainly a confusing time for me. I didn't want to talk to my folks about anything. I certainly didn't want to share my innermost thoughts with anyone at Saint Luke.

Once again, I was hearing the music. I remembered when a Christian group came to our school to do a show for the winter assembly when I was in sixth grade. They performed music from Godspell. I kept hearing the words in my head to Day By Day.

Chapter Seven
Battle Scars

When I got up the next morning, I immediately took a peek in the mirror. I had hoped that the evidence of love had miraculously disappeared overnight. "Shit!" There was no such luck. It looked worse. I remembered hearing some of the other kids talking about getting sucker bites in the past. I had thought that it might be hip to have some, but after my experience, I came to the conclusion that it was just stupid and embarrassing.

I mean, what is the logic behind such a thing? The sucker wants everyone to know that she is a vampire? The sucked wants to signal to everyone his rite of passage? Was it customary? Ceremonial? Actually, it sucked so much that I decided to go through my closet looking for coverage. I pulled out the ugly, shit, brown turtleneck shirt that I got for Christmas—the one that I swore I would never wear in public. It managed to cover up half of the mess. I decided to pretend that the rest of the marks were from a scuffle with one of the angry project kids.

I headed out the door. When I got to the end of my street—there was Ratboy. He seemed to have battle scars of his own, including a Band-Aid across his forehead. The funny thing was that he could walk into the school carrying his head and nobody would question it. The slightest alteration on my body would cause me to be questioned from everyone. That might have been the only advantage Chuck ever had. Everyone automatically expected him to look like hell, because he usually did.

"Chuck, what happened to you outside the church yesterday?"

"I fell down, why?"

"I thought Spencer might have done that to you."

"No, he…uh…told me to tell everyone that I fell down."

"What's in it for you—altar boy service?"

"He let me keep the money I borrowed from the church."

"Really? How much did you get?

"Twenty bucks."

When I heard that, I just stood there with my mouth agape. It was something that I needed to look into. Tony got paid to wear a ridiculous robe and light candles for Spencer. Ratboy was getting paid for being abused by the same guy. I wondered what I needed to do to get my share…or would it even be worth it?

"Chuck, do you want to go to the White Front after school to spend some of it?"

"I already spent all of it."

"Already? What did you get?"

"Some reefer."

"What's that? What did you say?"

"Nothing—I just spent it all. Don't worry about it, okay?"

I thought that I knew what Ratboy referred to when he said reefer. I remembered hearing that word before. I think it was also what Cathy meant when she asked me if I wanted to smoke something that she found in her brother's room when I was in her house the day before—something other than cigarettes. Ratboy was growing up fast—maybe a little too fast, and so was Cathy. It gave me a stomach ache just thinking about it.

When we walked past the hippie house, Ratboy waived at the two hideous monsters that were standing out on the porch. One of them had several scars on his face. He kind of looked like an older version of Ratboy. I imagined a public service announcement saying…this could be you in ten years, or…stay in school, or…crime doesn't pay. Ratboy's future may have been staring right at his scarred face. It may have been preordained.

As we were passing, one of the hippies yelled out with a gravelly sounding voice, "Do you need any more junk?"

Ratboy looked over toward the porch and shook his head. I didn't ask any other questions. Ratboy had been like a human danger zone most of his life. He lived on the fringes, and I often found it to be intriguing, but now I started to feel that perhaps it was getting to be a little too dangerous for me.

When we got closer to the schoolyard, I asked him, "Are you going to altar boy training on Saturday?"

"Yea, I'll be there. Are you going?"

"Yea, but I hope we won't be there all day. You know that our first game against Saint John is at Four o'clock, Chuck, right?"

"Yea, I won't be going there."

"What do you mean? Are you kidding me?"

"No…I quit the team."

I wasn't surprised to hear him say that because it made sense. He probably wouldn't have spent any time on the court, with the exception of the court located inside of the locker room that would usually find him guilty of something, and then the judges would execute a swift punishment for him. Besides, he had enough to keep himself busy with poor boxes, reefer, hippies and Father Spencer.

So, like many times in the past, we walked side by side through the yard and into the school. Ratboy wore his war wounds proudly. On the opposite end of the spectrum, I did what I could to cover up my love wounds. We were about as opposite as two kids could possibly be from each other. We somehow managed to get through the rest of the week without much more chaos…and then it was Saturday.

***

When Ratboy and I walked into the church on Saturday morning, we immediately noticed the two outfits that were lying on top of one of the front pews. I guessed that Spencer wanted us to look the part from the start. It helped to elevate the misery level for me. The gloom grew rapidly inside of me.

I didn't see Spencer anywhere. So, while I sized up my outfit, Ratboy was making his way toward the poor box again. I became slightly annoyed at the idea that he felt he was entitled to make a withdrawal whenever he wanted. It bothered me because I knew that my grandmother would occasionally part with the little bit of social security money that she had to make a generous deposit into what she must have assumed to be a security box.

I figured that Spencer was probably lurking somewhere in the vicinity. So I whispered, "Chuck." Then I waved him over. When he walked back toward me, I pleaded, "What…are you crazy or something? He's gonna catch you again. Don't be stupid."

"It's okay, Tom, he said that he would leave money in there for me if I did some favors for him."

"Are you serious? What kind of favors are you doing for him?"

Just then, Father Spencer walked out onto the altar. "Well, right on time—altar boy recruits."

Both of us said out of sync, "Good morning Father Spencer."

"Good morning to both of you. Now, go ahead and try on those cassocks."

Ratboy and I looked at each other dumfounded. It sounded like he said caskets. Then I pointed to the robes. "Father, do you mean these?"

"Yes—yes, go ahead and put them on."

Ratboy and I were about the same size, as were the two outfits. I tentatively grabbed the one that was closest to me, and Ratboy took hold of the other. We slipped them on over our street clothes, and we were ready to go. At least we looked the part…well kind of. Both of us could have used a good haircut. The nuns were always on our case about us growing our locks. At least our colors matched up with Spencer. We were a peculiar threesome.

Father Spencer went over all of the basics with us: ring a bell, light a candle, look stupid, and bring out the Eucharist, the wine, the water, the blood…. I think it was fake blood, but he always mentioned it in his sermons. He kept us busy doing a lot of insignificant little things that were customary and ceremonial.

There wasn't that much to it, but Ratboy kept screwing up anyway. After about two and a half hours, Father Spencer said,

"That's enough training for today, boys. If you two would like to stick around, I can use your assistance in the rectory."

He gave me a quick glance. I didn't think that he expected me to hang around. "Uh…I have to go home Father," I responded.

Then he looked at Ratboy with a more serious expression. It was more like Father was telling him to stick around instead of asking him, and Chuck simply nodded his head.

I started taking off the cassock, and I asked, "Should I just leave this here, Father?"

"No, take it home with you. Get used to wearing it, and practice everything I taught you. I'll see you next Saturday at the same time." While he was talking to me, I noticed that his right hand was resting comfortably on top of Ratboy's shoulder.

I grudgingly responded with, "Okay…I will." I looked at the cassock in my hands knowing full well that I would never wear it outside of the church. I didn't think that I would even bother putting it on a hanger, and how the heck did he expect me to practice at home anyway?

As I walked away, I noticed that Ratboy had an expression on his face that looked like he was thinking…maybe I shouldn't have quit the team, or possibly…maybe I didn't need the poor box money that badly. Whatever it was, it was based on his poor decisions. I was just glad to get the hell out of that so called heavenly place sooner than I had anticipated.

I went home to rest up for the game. When I got to my bedroom, I noticed that the sheets were removed from my bed. My mom must have decided that the linen needed its yearly washing. I set the cassock down on the bed as a substitution for the sheets, and I lay on top of it.

Four o'clock rolled around quick enough. It was the first game of our hopefully illustrious season, and we were playing on our home turf. I was happy to see that my love-bites had mostly faded away, so I was able to still look pretty good in my uniform while sitting on the bench. Coach Morgan always wore a heavy dose of Old Spice or Aqua Velva which complimented the stench coming from some of my teammates.

I watched our opponent—Saint John as they tried to warm up. They looked like a fairly uncoordinated bunch. They had a stupid looking hunchback kid on the team who was well over six feet tall. He also seemed to be lacking in the coordination area, but he was still a little bit intimidating. Everyone watched for him to dunk the ball during the pregame warmups, but he didn't even come close. He barely got two inches off of the ground.

Marty took over the game from the start, and by halftime, we were up by twenty-two points. It was going to be a slaughter, and the other team already looked battered and beaten. I thought that there was a good chance that I would get into the game. A few of the other second stringers had already gotten to play.

When there was about five minutes left in the final period, Coach Morgan pointed at me. "Get ready to go in at the next buzzer Richards."

My nervousness was getting the best of me. I think that only half of me wanted to go in, but the idea of making a basket was still a powerful motivator. As I walked onto the floor, I saw Cathy standing there smiling at me. Her cheerleader skirt looked shorter than the ones that the other girls were wearing. I kept looking at her smooth, bare legs. My nervousness started to subside. I thought it would be okay, but then I felt a cold sweat overcome me, and, of all things—some penis growth. I tried not to look at her anymore.

I forced myself to get my mind into the game. The ball was tossed to me at about half court. I awkwardly started dribbling the ball toward our hoop. I passed the ball to one of my teammates. He quickly threw it back to me. My confidence somehow grew, and I decided to make a drive toward the basket. When I got close, I leaped in the air and tried to lob the ball toward my intended goal.

The big goon stood in my way, and it was like crashing into a brick wall. I lost control of the ball and my body slammed to the hard floor. My elbow felt like it was severely scraped, and I got up feeling a bit dizzy. The sound of the whistle, combined with the noise of the crowd was hurting my head. I kept shaking it.

I heard the referee yell, "Foul—two shots! Then he helped me up. "Are you okay, son?"

"Uh-huh," I managed as he handed me the ball.

I stood at the foul line, and I looked down while dribbling the ball a few times. I noticed that a few drops of blood had dripped from my elbow down onto my shoe laces. My first free throw had missed the rim completely. I heard someone yell, "Come on, Tom—sink it! You can do it!"

I tried to measure the basket with the second throw. It hit the backboard, spun twice around the rim, and dropped in for a bucket.

I jumped up and down. It was the first point of my career, and we still had most of the season to go. Coach Morgan noticed the blood and took me out. He got no complaints from me. I was wounded, but I still had achieved my goal.

After the game, while I was changing in the locker room, I decided to do something that I never did after a game—take a shower. I felt that I was able to overcome my embarrassment. It was, after all, a rare game for me. I worked up a sweat, scored a point, and got bloody. If that wasn't enough, I had recently noticed a few tiny hairs sprouting down below.

Maybe I was ready to become a man. I felt like I was ready to take on all comers: six foot goons, Cathy, Spencer, nuns, hippies, project punks, and anyone else. All of a sudden, everything seemed easier. I felt like I was finally in the game.

When I walked out of the gym, there she was waiting for me again—my woman. Ironically, I felt more grown up since our last encounter, and she seemed a little less woman with her cheerleader outfit and her hair in pigtails. For the first time, I felt as if we were both on the same level. It seemed more innocent than it did before. There wasn't any rain, or umbrellas, or any need to hide anywhere. It was a pleasant change for two dedicated sinners.

When I approached her, she said, "Nice game, Tom," but this time, she hesitated for a moment to see if I would make a move. Then, without too much delay, she humbly asked, "Would you like to walk me home?"

This time, I instinctively grabbed her hand. "Let's go."

We walked and occasionally skipped our way to her house. We laughed and sang. I didn't ask her if anyone was home. I wasn't concerned about Jesus attacking me, or her brother beating on me. My self-assurance continued to grow.

When we got to her home, we sat on her rusty, old porch swing for a while. There wouldn't be any sneaking around, or cigarettes, or any new sucker bites. It was just a couple of innocent Catholic kids holding hands and kissing, and no tongues either. It felt more…normal. Was it also normal that my little fella seemed to be getting restless again? I tried to get him to settle down, but it wasn't that easy anymore.

We sat there watching the darkness overtake the sky. We were mostly silent while we listened to the old swing creaking as we went back and forth on it. It might have been a romantic moment. She paused for a moment to light a little candle that sat on a table next to her. She was fond of candles. I wondered if it was something that she…or her mom had picked up on from going to church so often.

As the candle flickered in the dark, her mom decided to come out on the porch to say hello. "Would you two like something to drink?" She asked.

At first I thought that she meant alcohol when I looked at her baggy eyes and weathered skin, while remembering her reputation for hanging out at the bar. We used to think she was Cathy's grandmother, but I remembered hearing that she didn't have kids until she was well into her forties. Then I came to my senses, and I thought of Nestles Quick again. I just shrugged and looked at Cathy who said, "Hot cocoa would be nice, mom."

At least we were thinking along the same lines. Unfortunately, Mrs. Davis wasn't thinking for herself. You could probably smell the booze on her breath if you were standing a quarter mile away, which was approximately the distance from her house to the entrance of the church…or the bar. Her hands were shaking when she brought out the two cups of cocoa, and I felt sorry for her when she burned one of her hands from a little spillage that dripped out of the overfilled cups. I guess that we all get scarred at some point, and usually when we aren't expecting it.

We sat there sipping the cocoa and giggling. I wondered if Cathy was officially my girlfriend yet. I was afraid to ask her. I never had one before. I wasn't sure how it worked. Was there a process? Did I need to ask permission? I would probably wait for her to decide. She was usually good at making the first move, but it was getting late, so any other romantic decisions would have to wait for another day.

When I left her house, I decided to walk past the gym on my way home. I wanted to see if anyone was still hanging around. When I got there, I noticed that the lights were still on and the door was left ajar. I peeped inside, and noticed that it was just the janitor finishing his cleaning duties.

Before I left, I stared at the trophy case for a minute. I imagined that there was a special award inside there for me. It had large gold lettering that read Congratulations Tom Richards for Scoring One Point in The 1974-75 Season. I kept staring through the glass until I heard a voice yell, "Hey—who's up there?"

I heard the janitor coming toward me, so instead of hanging around and explaining myself, I decided to scuttle my way out the door. As I continued my walk home, I also decided that I needed to try to score some more points...maybe a lot more.

Chapter Eight

Tricks…But No Treats

It was Halloween week at Saint Luke, and there were plenty of tricksters within the perimeter. During lunch period on Monday, Tony—who always seemed to be working on a comedy routine—came up to me and asked, "Tom, what kind of meat does a priest eat?"

"Uh…I don't know, man."

"None—get it?"

I didn't get it. I thought it was a terrible joke. I responded like I usually did when I didn't catch on to one of his lousy riddles. "Ha-ha! That's funny. Did you tell your brother?"

"Yea, but he didn't get it either."

It was like I was still having those déjà vu experiences, when, on the next day, Tony approached me once again and asked, "Tom, what kind of meat does a priest eat?"

"Uh…none?"

"No…n—u—n! Get it?"

This time I wasn't laughing, but he was—hysterically. I thought that perhaps there was something wrong with him. He was becoming a bit annoying, and I felt tempted to slug him one, but that thought quickly disintegrated when I saw big brother Mike approaching us.

Mike said to Tony, "Did you ask him?"

"Yea, but he didn't get the joke either."

"No, not that stupid joke…I mean about tonight—you know."

Tony was still laughing like a goof, so Mike said, "We're meeting tonight in the yard at seven o'clock."

"Why? What's going on, Mike?"

Tony and Mike kept looking at each other and smiling. I wondered if they were trying to set me up for something again. Tony finally stopped laughing and said, "Streaking."

I responded with, "What? What's that?"

Both of them started howling like mad men, and then Mike said, "Just be here around seven, okay? You'll see."

***

I showed up at seven o'clock just like Mike asked me…I mean, like he told me. He also said that he told a few other guys to be there too, but they didn't show up. Perhaps they had a better idea of what the gag entailed. We tossed a little Nerf football around the yard until it was perfectly dark. Then, Mike yelled. "Let's go! Let's do it now, guys!"

The three of us walked to the end of the schoolyard. Mike and Tony started taking off their shirts and pants. I stood there embarrassed while looking around uncomfortably. Tony said, "Come on—hurry up! Let's go!"

Still unsure of what I was getting into, I started to strip down anyway. A few seconds later, the three of us were standing there with nothing on but our shoes and socks. Then, the two brothers started jumping up and down and yelling like a couple of savages. Mike turned to me. "What's the matter, Tom? I thought you said that you were part Indian."

All of a sudden, Tony started running across the yard. Mike ran right behind him. I didn't want to be caught with my pants down, but I started to sprint anyway. We ran to the end of the yard and back, but we weren't done yet. We did a second lap, and then we committed to a third. I continued to go along with it. I hoped that the pre-Halloween *streaking* nightmare would end soon.

I kept thinking that if anyone saw me…or worse—got me on camera, they would lock me up with my Uncle Ted at Willow Grove. It was the kind of setting that they would place you in if they determined that something wasn't functioning properly in the brain area. Of course, I knew of a few other people that would be more at home there than I would ever be.

After going back and forth five times, the three, naked, little Catholic boys were quite winded. Then we noticed a set of headlights gleaming toward us from a side street that was adjacent to the school, and we instantly froze. I guess we weren't really expecting an audience. Maybe it was what a naked deer would feel like. We looked at each other. Mike was blushing, and I just felt weird.

"Who is that?" Tony whispered.

"I...uh...uh...don't know," Mike and I stuttered simultaneously.

So we decided not to push our luck any further. I was glad to find that my clothes were just where I left them with nobody else in sight...except for Saint Luke, of course. After I put my clothes back on, I lied to the Santino brothers by telling them I had to go home to do my homework. I just wanted to get out of there before they asked me to do something even more ridiculous.

I walked home thinking that I was glad that it was my last year at Saint Luke, and that I would hopefully make some new friends in high school. I became weary of hanging around with not only Ratboy, but the mafia brothers as well. When I went to bed that night, I had all of my clothes on including my shoes.

***

On Wednesday morning, just before first period, I noticed that Marty Monday was sneaking around the cloakroom. Curious to see what he was up to, I popped my head inside for a closer look. He appeared to be going through the pockets of several coats and jackets that were hanging on the rack. He stood close to where my jacket was hanging, so I stepped inside. "Hey, Marty, what's going on?"

He looked at me angrily. "Huh? …Nothing…just get out of here!"

I quickly walked out of the cloakroom. I didn't want to be involved in whatever dirty trick he was scheming. There wasn't anything in my jacket for him to steal anyway. I doubted if anyone else would have much for him to lift either.

I had been noticing that Marty was becoming more ornery, and a lot more aloof. I think that out of anyone in the school, he was perhaps the most mysterious, but he had plenty of competition.

The teacher didn't make an appearance yet, so Marty was still back there doing his thing. I decided to take another quick glance. This time he was going through a lunchbox. I recognized it, and it definitely wasn't his. It was Patricia Musgrove's pink, white, and maroon, Penelope Pitstop lunchbox. I wondered if he was so desperate as to steal someone's food. Unfortunately, it wasn't that simple, and I soon wished that I wasn't such a Peeping Tom.

Patricia was the weird, shy girl that everyone liked to make fun of. Her mother often walked her to school, and made most of the clothes that she wore. She never talked to any of the boys, rarely talked at all unless she responded to a teacher. To spare her any embarrassment, the teachers rarely called her name in class.

When I saw Marty unwrap her sandwich, spit in it, and then carefully rewrap it, I wished that I played hooky that day because it sickened me. After witnessing the horror, I just took my seat and tried to forget about the whole thing. I decided that Marty was not only a mystery man, but one of danger and deceit.

I tried not to look at Patricia all morning long, but it was an impossible task. She always looked so innocent with her pure white skin and even whiter stockings. I felt as if I wanted to tell her about it. But how could I? I just wanted the morning to pass by quickly, and I wanted to make sure that I was nowhere near her during lunch period. Maybe she wouldn't be hungry, or possibly she would have a stomach ache, or maybe she would accidentally drop her sandwich on the floor. I tried to rationalize the situation out of my head. Whatever guilt I felt, I hoped that Marty's was tenfold, but I had serious doubts about him having any kind of conscience at all. It would probably haunt me forever. I never told anyone about it. I thought that my lunch tasted lousy that day.

When I got to the schoolyard on Thursday morning, I saw Mike leaning against the school building and holding something that was wrapped up in a brown paper bag. It didn't look like it would be his lunch. As soon as he saw me, he waved me over to him. I had a feeling that another gag was in process.

As I approached him, he said, "We pitched in to get Mr. Knight something for Halloween — something that he really needs." He reached into the bag and pulled out a small bottle of green Listerine. "We need you to stick this in his desk when he's not looking."

"Why me? Why should I do it?" I asked timidly.

"Because he's your uncle — that's why. He'll just think it's a gift or something. Don't be such a pussy, Tom."

Mike handed me Uncle Joe's present, and I just kept staring at it. I probably was the best pigeon in the flock to make the delivery.

"Uh…okay…uh…what should I do with…?"

"Just stick it in his desk drawer when he is out of the classroom. It will be easy. You have to trust me, man."

I didn't trust him. I didn't trust anyone…anymore. "Okay…I'll do it."

I stuffed the gift into my book bag. Mike stuck out his hand for me to slap him five, and I grudgingly accommodated him. Then he slapped mine twice as hard and said, "My man."

Uncle Joe's bad breath was legendary. Every kid in the school knew of it, and so did all of the parents and the entire faculty. It was hard not to notice. Nobody ever wanted to stand close to him. I could remember once when he was talking to Jane Adams in the hallway. While she listened to him, she probably wasn't conscious of the fact that she was squeezing her nose. It was that bad. It could be rather nauseating on certain days. You had to develop a stomach for it.

Uncle Joe was my second period teacher. My mom told me to make sure that I had a seat in the front row to show him my respect. It was rather punishing at times. He was tough enough just to look at, and I often felt like I was enveloped in a stifling cloud of halitosis.

On the positive side, I did have a short journey to get from my desk to his. I strategically took the bottle of green mouthwash out of my book bag and placed it inside of my desk when his back was to us. I was ready to make my big move.

Mike sat a couple of rows behind me. He was ready to quarterback the play if necessary. We were waiting to see if Uncle Joe would need to leave the class for some purpose. If not, I would have to attempt to make the drop off between classes. Mike told me that a few other kids pitched in for the halitosis medicine. I suspected that it was solely financed by him.

With about ten minutes left to Uncle Joe's class, a familiar sound began to ring through the halls of Saint Luke. FIREDRILL!

As it was going off, I heard Mike's voice behind me saying, "Tom—Tom—do it! Do it now! Hurry up!"

Uncle Joe had stepped into the hall momentarily, but there wasn't enough time. When he walked back into the room, he requested,

"Okay, ladies and gentlemen—single file all the way out of the building. You know the drill." Then, he stood at the doorway waiting for the room to empty out. The drop off would have to wait until later.

It was the usual procedure that the school implemented at least twice a year: clear out the building in record time, do a thorough head count, and go back into the building once the smoke had cleared, but there was never a fire. There were never any fire trucks either. Marty once told me that he was going to set off the alarm for a joke. Ratboy told me that he thought about setting an actual fire. Neither of these events had taken place…yet.

As we were walking back into the school, I noticed that Ratboy was out of line. He was about thirty kids ahead of me. He was acting like a goof and talking to a couple of girls from the seventh grade. Goofing off was typical for him, but getting the attention of any of the female students was a rare phenomenon. Unfortunately, Uncle Joe caught wind of it, and by the expression on his face, he didn't like it one bit, especially during the fire drill when we were supposed to march in and out of the school like good little Nazis with no talking and absolutely no goofing off.

Uncle Joe started to make his way toward the rat. "Excuse me—excuse me, please," he said politely while shoving innocent children out of his way. He was in pursuit, and he looked about as angry as I remembered ever seeing him. His head was beet red and his veins were bulging above his eyebrows. It looked like his head was going to explode. I could have sworn that I heard him growling like a mad dog when he walked past me. I've seen less scary monsters at the Chiller Saturday matinees.

When he caught up to his target, he balled up his fist and cracked Ratboy in the back of the skull with a furious, concussion provoking swat. It was an exhibition of shear brutality. A lesser eighth grader may not have been able to absorb the blow. Ratboy didn't utter a word. After nearly collapsing onto the floor, he just straightened himself out and quietly walked back to the classroom. As usual, he took it like a man although brain damage could have been setting in at any time.

It was the second time that I saw Ratboy getting clobbered during a fire drill. I remembered in seventh grade when he tripped Sister Mary Catherine in the hallway during the drill, and she muscled him down on the ground and slapped both of his rat ears back. I'm not sure if he even tripped her on purpose; he never admitted it to me.

After observing this most current act of cruelty, it helped to give me the strength to carry on with my task. I didn't want him to be my uncle anymore. I wondered if there was a process that I would have to go through to get him removed as being a relative to me. I would have to worry about that later. At the moment I needed to focus on completing my current mission.

By the time I got back to the classroom, Uncle Joe was still lingering at the other end of the corridor. While still nervous, I immediately went for his desk. I wasn't satisfied to just drop off his surprise gift. I started rooting through some of the personal items that he kept inside of the top drawer.

There was a glossy magazine lying amongst some test papers. I just glanced at it quickly while figuring that I might be running out of time. When I sat back at my desk, I immediately flashed back to the magazine. I was fairly certain that there was a picture of a large naked man on the cover, and I think the title of the publication was Big Balls and Ass.

I wondered why he would be in possession of such a thing. Was it confiscated from a student?—Doubtful. Was it part of an assignment?—Really doubtful. I thought back to a conversation that I overheard my parents discussing about how Uncle Joe always wanted to be a priest, but he wasn't qualified for some reason. I hated the fact that I was related to him.

Being so deep in thought, it took me a while to realize that I was the only person sitting in the classroom. That was because the fire drill ran past the allotted time for Uncle Joe's class. I started running out of the room while exclaiming my least favorite adult word, "Sh—It!"

On Friday, after school let out, some of the boys and I hung around the yard for a game of handball. It was a warm Indian summer like afternoon, and we figured that we wouldn't get too many more good opportunities before the cold winter set in. It was also November First—a.k.a.—All Saints' Day. I thought that perhaps all of the tricks were now behind us, but I knew that another little caper could be just a stone's throw away.

Our unofficial game of handball consisted of the pitcher tossing a rubber ball to an opposing player who stood at an imaginary home plate. The player would try to hit the ball as hard as he could with the front of his fist to try to make it go over the top of the twelve foot cement wall and into the alley. You either got a homerun or you got nothing. If you were too weak, you were better off not playing, at least not on Mike or Marty's team.

We played for a couple of hours, until most of the honest kids had to go home. There were five of us that decided to hang around: Ratboy, Mike, Marty, Calvin Gregory, and myself. There was a lot of scheming that went on in each of our heads.

We decided to take a break from the game, and the five of us took a walk down to the White Front. It was the name we gave to the little grocery store near the school because of the white awning that covered the entrance way. I don't think the store had an official name. While inside, Mike, Calvin, and I were buying a round of Pepsi at the counter. At the same time, Ratboy and Marty were loading up their coat pockets with Twinkies, Ho Hos, barbecue chips, and whatever else they fancied. They walked out of the store weighing a couple extra pounds each. Neither of them seemed nervous about it. It was like a normal procedure for the two thick thieves.

We all met back at the front steps of the school where we scarfed down the refreshments, and then we left all of the discards on the steps. Judging by all of the empty bags and wrappers that were lying on the ground, I would estimate that Marty and Ratboy beat the White Front out of at least ten dollars of merchandise. The robbers made sure that they shared the stolen goods with the rest of us, so that we all could share in the lack of guilt. None of us had the decency to toss any of the rubbish into the trash can that Ratboy leaned against.

The sun began to set, so we decided to get in one last round of handball. About a half hour into the game, Mike walloped the ball harder than I had ever seen it hit before. It easily skyed the top of the wall, bounced through the alley, over a fence, and into one of the yards.

We all went up to the alley to make a rough calculation of the distance. When Ratboy spotted the ball in the yard, he shouted, "Man, you hit that into Mr. Nice Guy's yard!"

Mike replied, "So what…go get it dumb-ass!"

Ratboy responded, "If I try to get that ball, he'll send out his German Shepherd to get my balls!"

Mike angrily asked, "Then why do you call him Mr. Nice Guy, dumb-fuck?"

"That's what my dad always used to call him."

"Your dad must be a dumb-ass too then. Everyone knows that he's a fall down drunk."

It was a low blow, but Mike had no shame. Everyone hesitated for a moment. Then I said, "I'll go get it."

I jumped over the fence to retrieve the game ball, but there was barely enough light to find it. I kept looking at the front of his house, so if I was spotted, I would quickly run for the fence before his German Shepherd would get to me. Ratboy told me that he was once bitten. He also said that he heard Mr. Nice Guy would add hot sauce onto the dog's food to make him extra mean and vicious.

The ball was lying next to Mr. Nice Guy's little garden, which was well depleted being so late into the year. Gracing the outside of the garden were many colorful little stones of various shapes and sizes. I threw the ball back to the guys, and then I loaded up my hands with the pretty stones.

I walked back toward the fence. "Look at these, guys."

Everyone looked enthralled by the magical stones as they each grabbed a few from my palms. It was now completely dark. The handball game was definitely over with, and we either needed to find a new game, or it was time to go home.

***

The first stone throw was initiated by Marty, and it went through the third window from the left on the second floor. We all looked at each other in amazement. The laughter soon erupted while all of the other stones were becoming restless in each of our hands.

Mike yelled, "Which one do you think is Sister Mary Catherine's classroom. Is it that one?" Then he just threw indiscriminately.

I think most of us made at least one toss that ended in a crash. Even though he was the least coordinated of the group, Ratboy was somehow able to most accurately hit his targets. He must have hated the school the most. I wasn't positive that Calvin made a wish with any of his wonder stones, but the other three demons and I left plenty of evidence inside of Saint Luke.

After about eight broken windows, we heard a voice yell, "Hey, what are you kids doing over there?" It was Mr. Nice Guy. He was standing under his back porch light with his killer mutt in tow.

"Get the hell out of here!"

We decided to split the scene. The other guilty parties and I went one way, and Calvin decided to distance himself by going in the other direction. Always having a song ready for every occasion, I instinctively started chanting the words to "No More Mr. Nice Guy", and of course, adding my own lyrics. "Let's get out of this scene—scene—scene."

By the time we made it to the end of the alley, reality had started to sink in. I didn't suspect that any of us were naïve enough to think that we would get away with our little trick. Come Monday morning there wasn't going to be any treats waiting for any of us either, but perhaps…our righteous deserts?

Chapter Nine
Crime Fighters

Soon after I left the scene of the crime on Friday evening, reality once again reared its ugly head. I almost forgot that Ratboy and I were scheduled for altar boy duty in our first Sunday mass service. That meant that there would be a good opportunity for the school to interrogate the two of us first—regarding the window breakings.

Our senseless vandalism was all I thought about the entire day on Saturday. On Sunday morning, I got my mom to iron my wrinkled cassock and trim my hair. I thought that it would help to make me look more innocent. As I left my house, I sensed that it was going to be one nerve-wracking day of prayer, but I did my best to remain as calm possible.

There was a full congregation waiting inside of the church for noon mass to start. Nothing was said to me about the windows upon my arrival, so I just went about my business as if nothing happened. I thought that Ratboy must have been a little more nervous when I witnessed him trip over his feet upon his first appearance on the altar. The audience gasped while I stood there shaking my head. The sleeve of his robe had caught on fire from one of the altar candles, and he was waving his arm in the air in an attempt to put it out. As much as I hated the job, I still wanted to give an impression that I was the more professional out of the two of us. Ratboy made that easy.

I saw my grandmother sitting in a pew in the first row. She looked at me with a warm smile that I interpreted as her saying what a wonderful grandson I have. I could sense my cheeks were getting red with embarrassment. I was sweating again. I was sure that grandma would never suspect my evil ways.

The cassock was useful as a good cover to hide my sinful nature. It did make me appear less evil. There was a point during the mass when I imagined that I was the Pope, and everyone would stare at me in awe and then start throwing money at me. If I was the prima donna, I would also be able to keep Spencer in line.

Other than Ratboy's escapades, I thought that it worked out pretty well over all. I was semi-proud of my halfhearted performance. It felt as if my soul was uplifted. I even started familiarizing myself with some of the hymns like the somewhat joyous Hosanna in the Highest! I was able to find a bit of inspiration in almost any type of song, but I doubt if I would being singing any of those lyrics outside of the church walls.

I left the church shortly after the mass was completed. Ratboy was told to stay there. Once again, Father Spencer had a little *paying* job for him. The good Father didn't give me any cash, but I did pocket two dollars from my proud grandma. It was two less dollars that she could have put into the wooden box or the metal baskets that were passed around. Two less dollars that would have wound up in the clutches of the sinister Spencer or his halfwit, sidekick — Ratboy.

As soon as I got outside, I was tempted to return to the scene of Friday's crime to see if the windows were still broken. I could hardly believe that I wasn't questioned by Spencer or by one of the nuns that attended mass. Did they not know about it yet? Was I above suspicion? Or…was Sunday reserved for a day of prayer, and Monday for a day of reckoning. The ugly truth would continue weighing heavily upon my boney shoulders.

As I walked along the side of the church, I heard a voice shout out, "Mr. Richards!"

I turned to the left, and standing in front of the convent was the extremely stout figure of one Sister Mary Catherine. I tried to keep my distance this time. "Hi, Sister Mary Catherine," I nearly yelled.

"Can you please come here for a minute Mr. Richards?"

"Yes, Sister."

I walked toward her with a solemn expression, figuring that it couldn't be too good, but to my surprise she asked, "Can you assist me in moving a few boxes? It should only take a few minutes."

My spirit was again lifted as I responded, "Yes—sure—uh-huh."

It was my first trip inside of the convent. I was somewhat interested in seeing what it was like inside. I often wondered if their accommodations were as plush as Spencer's appeared to be when I visited the rectory a few times in the past.

When I walked inside, I was surprised to see that it was a dark, drab, and empty looking place with only a few pieces of furniture scattered about. It looked more like the school than it did the rectory. It made me wonder what they were doing with all of the loot, or if maybe Spencer controlled all of the money that came into the school and church.

There were about eight boxes, which by coincidence was also the number of windows we broke, sitting in what I perceived to be the dining room. I carried each box into an even emptier looking room without asking any questions regarding its contents.

I wondered why she would even need me for such a task, knowing full well that she was much stronger than I was—judging by the incident when she lifted me in the air and slammed my weak body into the blackboard when I forgot my homework. I suspected there was more for me to know, but I just continued to play along.

She stood there watching me carry each box, and not uttering a word. I thought that perhaps—like Spencer with Ratboy—she wanted a little Catholic boy slave for her own. If that was the idea, I didn't like it one bit. I just wanted to get it over with. My feet started moving quicker. I wanted to finish the job as soon as possible.

What was strange about the whole affair was that my penis was getting harder, but I wasn't certain why. It couldn't be because of her, I hoped. She weighed two hundred pounds. She had a musty smell to her. She looked like a man—chin whiskers and all. She wasn't a very sexy thing.

I tried to get my mind on something else, but as I carried the last box, I started to fantasize about seeing her naked, tree trunk legs. I wanted to see the hairy beast that hid under several layers of cloth. I wanted her to squeeze the life out of me with those fat legs, and make me pay for my sins. I wanted the ferocious beast to tame me. She could even be the hero, and I could be the damsel…or the damned in distress. I was on my way to becoming a very perverted young man. I felt doomed as I avoided making eye contact with her.

When I finished carrying the last box, I uneasily walked up to her with a small bulge in my crotch and asked, "Anything else, Sister Mary Catherine?"

She stared at me for a moment. It was as if she was trying to see right through me. I waited for her to ask me either…was that you who broke the windows? Or…were you thinking of fornication in my presence? Instead, she just said, "No—that will be all. You can go home now, Mr. Richards."

I simply nodded and walked away. I didn't even get a thank you from her. It was as if she determined that it was my duty to serve her, like if it was all part of my unpaid altar boy job, but just as I walked out the door I heard her utter, "I will remember you in my prayers…Mr. Richards."

I was just glad to get out of there unscathed, especially when I figured that Spencer would have plenty for Ratboy to do to fill up his afternoon. As I was leaving, I glanced across the walkway that separated the convent from the rectory, and I wondered whether my friend was being questioned about his possible role regarding the property damage. If not, then what exactly was Spencer doing with him all that time…and the other times?

On Monday morning, it was just what I expected. We were brought to Sister Ann Margaret's office one at a time for a round of lie detecting. I figured that either an eye witness such as Mr. Nice Guy came forward, or…I got ratted out from someone in our own ranks, or I just looked guilty enough.

On the other hand, it wasn't nearly as bad as I thought it would be. Neither Uncle Joe, Spencer, nor any of the other nuns were there to lean on us. There weren't any beatings or harsh treatment of any kind. It was like we were just going through the motions to make it all official. They wanted to let us know that they knew, and to remind us that we were always being watched by someone…somewhere.

When it was my turn in the static chair, Sister Ann Margaret stared me down for a moment, and then said with a rather soft voice, "I know that you were one of the window vandals. Your parents will have to pay for your share of the damages. Bring the money to me once you have it. Now, go back to your class."

I wondered just how much money that would be, but I didn't ask her anything. I didn't admit to anything. She didn't ask me for a response either. I knew I was guilty. She knew I was guilty. When you know — you just know. I figured that my folks would get a phone call at some point. I would get an earful from them. I would, of course, deny any participation, and I would let the adults work everything out. I would just dance my way around it like I did everything else.

The funny thing was that the phone call would never be placed. I wouldn't get an earful from anyone. The folks didn't need to pony up a nickel. The hierarchy at Saint Luke was a shrewd group. They would scare the bejesus into us for either their own personal amusement or for a general show of power, but profit would always be a motivator.

I guess they figured that if none of us punks showed up with the cash, they really didn't want to call our hard working folks and try to extort more cash out of them after already soaking them for overpriced tuition costs just a few months earlier. They had a much better and easier plan in the works.

It turned out that the windows were well insured. The school administrators were in cahoots with a local glass installer that was also a devout member of the church. The straight dope on this was that he would give the school a highly inflated estimate for the work, which they would send in to their insurance company. The insurance company would send a hefty check to the contractor who in turn would make a generous donation back to the school. Like that famous writer wrote, all's well that ends well.

Now, when school let out the following Friday, we had no interest in playing handball, or breaking windows, or robbing the White Front. Nope. It was our homecoming basketball game against the Fairies of Saint Mary's—our biggest rival for years. We always figured that they were a bunch of sissy boys, but they were also good ball handlers and, at least, average shooters. They beat us three out of the last four times we played them. It would usually be a tight game, and it was unlikely that I would get an opportunity to expand on my one point season total.

The game started out at a frenetic pace. Each team wanted to quickly gain the upper hand. We scored first, but they kept matching us basket for basket. There was a lot of shooting. There was a lot of fouling. There was a lot of sweating…even a little bit of swearing.

The score remained close throughout the game, with the lead changing hands several times. With about one minute left and the game tied, Mighty Marty was fouled while attempting a jump shot. The opposing player inadvertently smacked Marty on the side of his face. Marty took offense to it, and he shoved the Saint Mary fouler down to the floor. A few other players from both sides joined in, and an ugly brawl ensued.

Several other players and coaches from both teams joined in the melee. I never left my seat, but just about everyone else did, including several agitated parents and a few other spectators. I had never seen anything like it before. I'm sure that Saint Luke and Saint Mary were looking down on it all in pity.

All of a sudden, I heard a voice yell out from the bleachers, "Get 'em Batman. Get 'em Robin!"

There were at least fifty people on the gym floor during the skirmish. I started scanning through the crowd while trying to determine who the spectator was referring to when he yelled out to egg on the two masked…or unmasked crime fighters.

When I saw tall, lean mean Father Spencer—clothed in all black—slug a parent from the other squad, and Uncle Joe—wearing his more colorful threads—pushing everyone back to their seats, it all became abundantly clear who the spectator was referring to.

It was a once-in-a-lifetime spectacle. The smile on my face grew large. The game almost didn't matter anymore. I had come to the realization that I loved all of violence. I especially liked that I didn't have to lift a finger to make it possible. For a brief moment, I loved Father Spencer. I adored Uncle Joe. I even idolized Marty. Three people that in most other circumstances, I had a disdain for.

When the floor finally cleared out, the coaches decided to play out the last few seconds that remained in the game. We lost the game by one point, and Father Spencer's Cadillac was referred to as the Batmobile from that day forward.

Now, all of the characters were in place at Saint Luke. We had Batman and Robin. The Penguin could have been any one of the nuns. Mike was the Joker. Tony was The Riddler. Cathy had to be Catwoman. Marty could be Mr. Freeze. Ratboy was one of the henchmen that got beat-up in the fight scenes when you would see words on the screen like POW! BAM! ZOKK! Me? I just wanted to watch and be entertained, and I loved that title song too.

Chapter Ten
Keep Off the Grass

On a late November afternoon, as I walked home from school, I noticed that Ratboy was sitting all alone on a metal railing that supported the steps along the Layers. The combination of the crisp autumn air and the cigarette that he was smoking created a large cloud all around him.

As I approached him, a musky scent entered my airspace. It was familiar but not too familiar. I remembered a similar odor when I walked past the hippie house on a few occasions. Ratboy would take a deep inhale, and then he would make a funny expression on his face as he exhaled. The cigarette looked fat in the middle and skinny at the ends like it was crudely wrapped. I remembered when he told me that his father would sometimes make his own cigarettes in order to save money.

After several, of what appeared to be painful, puffs, he turned to me. "Do you want a hit, dude?"

I thought about how Ratboy was increasingly coming out with his own lingo. He called it project slang. I remembered how my throat burned the last time I tried to smoke a cigarette with Cathy, but this seemed different. It looked different. It smelled a lot different. Then, the thick cloud was around both Ratboy and me. He seemed to be on a cloud of his own.

I felt as if I was getting dizzy just from the smell. "What is it?"

"Just take a toke already, old man. Here…take it," he said as he handed it to me.

I took a small puff. It tasted harsh…or more like…bitter sweet. I took a bigger drag. Then I took another, and I felt a huge rush shooting up to my brain. It was an exhilarating, yet spooky feeling. I kept looking at the cigarette in my hand. For a moment I thought that I was looking at two cigarettes and eight or nine fingers.

"Don't Bogart that joint, man! Give it back to me!" Ratboy shouted at the top of his lungs.

I snapped out of it, right back to reality.

After I handed it back to him, he started inhaling its smoke through his nose. Then he took another big drag, and exhaled the smoke in small sequences. Puff…puff…puff. It was almost artistic. It seemed like someone had given him private lessons to perfect this art. It was the first time that I had ever seen him do anything with any kind of expertise. He seemed to be comfortably within his element. He had a rather proud yet somewhat dopey look on his face. Ratboy was involved with something new that most of the other kids at Saint Luke knew nothing about.

"So, what is this stuff?" I asked.

He responded, "It's dope—you dope. What did you think it is?"

The last time I heard the term was when I was watching television and there was a public service announcement warning kids to stay away from it. On top of that, how could Ratboy have the audacity to call anyone a dope? He wasn't exactly the Pope.

Then I asked, "You mean dope like in…uh…."

"Yea…dope…weed…grass…Mary Jane…reefer…pot." He was a walking talking dope dictionary. He slung a lot of slang.

Still being unsure of what I was getting into, but trying to be hip, I said, "Yea, sure, I know pot." I just hoped that my life wasn't going to it the way his was.

Ratboy kept toking away. He noticed the nervous expression on my face. "Just be cool—fool. Take another hit—tit."

Ratboy never talked or acted quite like that in my presence before. He kept coming up with silly rhymes. He must have been hanging around with a different crowd. We weren't loafing together as much as we used to either. He was developing a whole new personality. It was like a Ratboy Renaissance.

I had to ask, "So, how do you get this…dope?"

"I bought it. What do you think?"

"Does it cost a lot? Where did you get the money? Can I buy some of it?"

I kept asking a lot of questions, but he wouldn't provide the answers to most of them. He would just look at me with a smirk. He probably didn't want to admit that he was either stealing the money or getting it from doing favors for Spencer. I'm sure that he was still making withdrawals from the poor box. I thought that maybe he should keep his hands out of that box and spend more time in the confession box, but probably not with Spencer. Of course, if he did, then perhaps the two of them could trade off their sins with each other. He could always spend time in the booth with Father Murphy. We didn't have much dirt on him yet.

On the other hand, Ratboy may have been better off sneaking into an entirely different church where his criminal activity was not yet known. Although, they would probably soon notice that their weekly donation amounts would start to slip, and maybe they would be even less lenient with him. He would have to find a new church every month. Lucky for him there were many to choose from.

We lived in the land of churches. There was one on almost every block. I wondered if it was a coincidence that there was also a bar on nearly every block. If I had a dollar to bet, I would wager that Cathy's mom wasn't the only devout church member in town that helped keep the bar business going. She just couldn't hide her alcoholism quite as well as some other people could.

The marijuana joint didn't have a filter on it. Ratboy kept smoking it until it got so small that it looked like it was burning his fingers. Then he pulled out of his pocket what he referred to as a roach clip, which kind of resembled a pair of tweezers with teeth. He held the roach at the end of the clip while snorting and inhaling it until it completely disappeared. I thought that it was the perfect ending: Ratboy inhaling a roach. I just stood there watching in reverence.

A few minutes later, I started to feel lightheaded. The combination between the pot and the platform shoes that I started wearing again made me feel like I was at least a foot taller. I felt like I was swaying back and forth as if I was sailing on the Pittsburgh Clipper in rough waters. I felt like I was on top of the US Steel building on a windy day.

Ratboy looked at me. "Man, your high as a fucking kite!"

He seemed to be taking it all in quite well. I only took a few hits, and I felt the effects. Ratboy bathed his lungs and nostrils with the poisonous chemical, but he was obviously a veteran. It didn't seem to be affecting him anywhere near as much.

As I started gaining back my equilibrium, I went into stage two—Silliness. The world appeared distorted to me. Everything seemed so comical. I started howling at some of the degenerates that walked past us. I wasn't afraid of them anymore, and they didn't bother me. It was like I had a protective coat on…or I was invisible…invincible. I thought they all resembled some type of creature. One guy reminded me of a walrus, another guy was like a rooster. Even Ratboy looked like...well...a large rodent? I didn't need to be too high for that vision. It made me laugh until I choked.

When I finally got over my fit, I moved into stage three—Queasiness. I had to sit down for a while. It didn't take long for me to barf on Ratboy's pants and shoes. He wasn't angry about it either. I guess that he felt responsible for the deadly toxin that inhabited my being, or maybe he was just fascinated by the multi-colored puke. He just stood up and tried to shake off some of the loose vomit from the bottom of his bellbottoms.

I felt as if we had temporarily reversed roles. Ratboy looked like he felt sorry for me instead of the other way around. He was also much more in control of the situation than I was. When he got bored observing me sitting there staring into space like a simpleton, he just said, "Take it easy, man," and walked away.

I didn't want to go home because of the condition I was in and because of the reefer-vomit stench that I would carry into my house. I just sat there for as long as I could in order to clear my head as well as the smoky air that still circulated around me.

I remembered staring at some red ants that were crawling near my feet for the longest time. Then I figured that I must have been imagining it because the ants wouldn't survive the temperature by the time of year that it was, but I just kept looking at them until they crawled away. I must have been in stage four—Hallucination.

When the insects finally disappeared from my sight, a shadow had taken their place. There was someone standing in front of me. Actually, there were four people standing in front of me. I recognized three of them: Sister Ann Margaret, Father Spencer, and Uncle Joe. Could this be trouble? I pondered. I just stared into what could have been someone's terrible interpretation of Wonderland.

Sister Ann Margaret said abruptly, "Mr. Richards, do you think this is proper attire for a good Catholic boy?" Uncle Joe kept shaking his head, and Spencer was...licking his lips for some reason. I recalled having much happier nightmares in the past.

The fourth person wore funny-looking, vintage style clothing like if he was from another era. He almost looked royal. He had a heavy beard, wings, and what looked like a faint halo above his head. I figured that it had to be either Saint Luke or one of the doped out hippies. Then I noticed that he had two extra appendages protruding from his sides, and I thought that he could be an alien.

I couldn't make any sense of the whole thing. Why were they all there together? School had let out several hours earlier. The school was a half mile away. Did I forget my homework again? I kept shaking my head and blinking my eyes. I was hoping that they would all soon disappear. My body felt as if it was on fire.

Then I thought about what Sister Ann Margaret said about my attire, and why Spencer may have been licking his lips. I looked at myself and noticed that I was...naked! Well, not totally, I still had my clip-on tie attached to the skin on my chest, and my shoes and socks were still on. It wasn't proper attire for anything or anywhere, except for maybe…streaking.

As I continued to try to make sense out of everything, the four of them started laughing loudly. I glanced back toward them and they looked ghastly…or maybe…ghostly. The laughing kept increasing in volume. I had to cover my ears to try to mute the horrible laughter, but it got even louder. I looked back down to the ground to try to visualize the crawling ants again, but they weren't any help. They must have gone back to their colony.

I felt like I would begin to weep. I wanted my mommy. Then, from behind me, I felt a hand grasp my right shoulder. I turned around quickly and saw that it was my neighbor — Barney Lesko. He was speaking, but I couldn't make out any words that he was saying.

I shook my head a few times, and I noticed that the laughter had stopped. The four people that were standing in front of me had disappeared in the mist, and I was glad to see that I had all of my clothes back on. I must have dozed off for a while.

I looked back at Mr. Lesko. His hand was still on my shoulder, and he asked, "Are you alright, kid? Are you okay?"

"Yea…I'm ok. I was just…r — resting for a while. I'm alright."

My voice sounded slower and deeper than normal. It felt like I had just gotten past my puberty stage along with the some of the dope stages. I could have been in the Twilight Zone. It looked like the sun had recently set.

As he started walking away, he said, "You don't want to hang around here after dark. Some of those potheads congregate around here, you know."

It sounded like a premonition. "Yea, I do know. Thanks…dude."

He glanced back at me. "What? What did you say?"

"Uh…nothing, thanks, Mr. Lesko."

I looked up to the sky and noticed that a full moon was already visible. I lifted myself up off the ground. I had to move slowly because both of my feet had fallen dead asleep, along with my head. I started walking home while thinking about Mr. Lesko's excellent advice.

I thought back to when I played football with a few friends in my backyard over the summer. The ball had accidently gone into Mr. Lesko's yard a few times. Each time I would make a daring jump over his fence to retrieve it. He didn't like any of us going onto his property. He was too proud of it. The next day he erected a big sign that read KEEP OFF THE GRASS. It could have had more than one meaning to it. He was familiar with the yard jumpers as well as some of the local potheads. He was the neighborhood busybody.

I always thought that it would be a breakout year for me, but if someone would have told me that I would have turned into a dope head, sexual pervert, vandal, and altar boy all within the last few months of Nineteen Seventy-four, I would have thought that they were cracked in the skull...or on dope.

None of this was my fault, of course. My behavior was fueled by the constant negative element that surrounded me. It was either Ratboy's fault or the Santino boys were to blame. Marty was a bad influence on me as were Cathy, Spencer, Uncle Joe, and even some the Sisters. I decided that if anything awful would ever happen to me for the rest of my life, I would blame one of them.

I was able to rationalize myself into a fairly comfortable position. I didn't have to blame myself for anything anymore. I could either blame it on my mentors at Saint Luke, or figure that it was just peer pressure from some of the little demons that always seemed to be around me.

At the same time, I knew that I definitely didn't want to be like any of them. Being occasionally influenced was one thing, but being impressed to the point that it would change my outlook was something else. There were dangerous signs all around. There was cruelty and perversion lurking in the shadows.

I didn't remember ever being that deep in thought before. Once again, I wasn't paying attention to where I was walking. I didn't notice that I had stepped in a stinking heap of dog shit. I also didn't realize that I walked nearly a block past my house. It wasn't my fault. It was the dope. Ratboy was the culprit.

I finally snapped out of it when I started smelling the canine waste that was beneath the soles of my shoes. I thought that it might at least cover up the reefer scent, but I still scraped off the bottom of my shoes on the street curb anyway. I would attempt to clean my soles as well as cleanse my soul the best I could before I went into my house.

As I turned around and started my walk back home…all of a sudden everything seemed wonderful in my universe. I waved to a few neighbors that I saw, and I started humming a familiar tune. I had moved into the final stage—Happiness. With everything that happened, I still didn't have a worry in the world, unlike some others that I knew.

As soon as I arrived at home, I went straight for the bathroom. I needed to find a good cover for my horrendous dope-vomit breath before the folks noticed it. When I opened the medicine cabinet, I saw an unopened, small bottle of green Listerine glaring at me. It was identical to the one I left in Uncle Joe's desk for the Halloween gag.

I shut the cabinet door, and looked at myself in the mirror. My eyes looked bloodshot. I wanted to make sure that I wasn't still dreaming. I kept moving my face closer to the mirror. I appeared different than I remembered the last time I posed in front of the glass. I seemed to look older. I started noticing every little feature on my face and neck: a few freckles, a mole, a pimple? I thought that I could still faintly see one of Cathy's sucker bites and Sister Theresa's hand print.

Everything looked more noticeable. I even started rooting through my scalp. I wasn't sure if I was looking for lice from spending so much time around Ratboy, or if I was looking for three sixes imbedded in my skull.

I must have examined myself in the mirror for a half an hour. Then I opened the cabinet again. I grabbed the mouthwash and twisted open the cap. I took a quick swig, and I almost vomited again. I decided — like Uncle Joe probably did — that perhaps it wasn't worth the trouble.

While I was lying in my bed that night, I wondered if there was some other mischief that I could get into before the end of the year. As my eyes were getting heavier, I wondered if I could go all the way with Cathy Davis. I wondered if I could score some pot from Ratboy. I wondered if....

Chapter Eleven

'Tis the Season

The chaos seemed to slowdown as we got closer to the holy Christmas season. Part of the reason was the early arrival of the bitterly cold weather that kept us from spending as much time outdoors, but the main reason was... that no one wanted to be a bad boy so close to the holidays?

I felt like I was on a good luck streak. I didn't get into much trouble at all considering the amount of mischief that I got involved with almost daily: reefer, broken windows, sex, streaking, forgotten homework, church incidents, etc. I didn't even hear anything else about Uncle Joe's mouthwash gift. For the time being, I was in the clear.

We would eventually get used to the winter wonderland. The falling snow would make it tempting to venture out. There would be jolly sled rides down Mannicort Hill. There would be vicious snow ball fights around the school. There would be days that the school would have to shut down because of the heavy accumulation.

On the final day before our Christmas break, the school decided to let us have a party during the third period in each classroom. We would have a gift grab bag, and everyone could bring in treats to snack on. Sister Ann Margaret said that if we all behaved like good little Catholic boys and girls, we might be able to go home early for the day.

Sister Theresa was my third period teacher, and even she was less Nazi-like when it got close to the Christmas or Easter seasons. I thought that I witnessed her cracking a smile for the first time ever that morning. It might have just been the angle of my view and the poor lighting overhead that made it appear as a smile. It was like looking at a much less attractive Mona Lisa. To everyone's surprise she brought in a large bag of Hershey's kisses to pass out to each of us. I think it was the only time in my life that I ate stale chocolate, but I was always told that it was the thought that counted.

Well, it all started out innocent enough. That was until Sister Theresa stood in front of the class and announced, "I have to visit Sister Ann Margaret for a few minutes. I want you all to be on your best behavior, okay class?"

"Yes, Sister Theresa," we all replied in well-timed unison.

I think I would have to blame it all on the cupcakes. Patricia Musgrove's mom must have thought that her daughter should try to win over some friends, so she gave her chocolate cupcakes that were topped with vanilla icing and colorful sprinkles to bring in for everyone. They sure looked pretty. The problem was that there were way too many of them and they tasted like dung. I remembered hearing that her mom was blind in one eye. Perhaps she had confused salt for sugar, or baking soda for flour.

The always thoughtful Marty started off our Christmas bash by tossing one of the cupcakes across the room and bashing Patricia in the back of her skull with it. It wasn't as bad as the time he spit on her sandwich, but it was enough to bring her to tears, and just like the window breaking incident, when Marty makes the first toss—others will surely follow.

In a matter of a minute, all of the uneaten cupcakes, and most of the other leftover food, were either splattered into the blackboard, smeared into the walls, scattered over the floor, or most of us were wearing it. Calvin Gregory had four cupcakes that were smashed into both sides of his eyeglasses. Veronica Dorsey's big boobs were another target.

While most of the kids were throwing, ducking, laughing, or crying, I noticed that Mike Santino was standing in front of a window in the back of the classroom. It looked like he was holding something out of the window. By the way he exerted himself, it appeared to be something rather heavy.

As I approached him, I noticed that the something was someone. He was holding little Mason Schrader by his ankles, and letting him twist about in the cold winter wind! Mason, nicknamed Fidget was the smallest kid in the eighth grade—even smaller than any of the girls. His dad was a nearly famous horse jockey. He was an easy target for Santino to prey upon.

Little redhead Mason yelled, "Let me go! Let me go!"

I thought—no, don't let him go! Don't let him go! We are three stories up!

Mike yelled, "Where's the dollar you owe me—you little dwarf?"

"I don't have any money," cried Mason.

I thought that even if he did have money, it would have likely fallen out of his pockets while he was hanging upside down, and the cash would be lying way down below on the schoolyard.

Mike continued harassing him. "I'll bring you back in if you give me two dollars tomorrow, Fidget."

Before Mason could answer, I heard a much louder voice coming from the front of the classroom. "You rotten little heathens!"

It was Sister Theresa. For the moment, her face looked like it was made of stone, and regardless of the angle of my view or the lighting, there was no possibility of a smile this time. She looked less and less like the Mona Lisa and more and more like the Fuhrer. The food that was splattered around the room resembled an amateur painter splattering paint on his canvas and getting a lot of it on himself and everything around him.

I don't think that Sister Theresa noticed Mike pulling little Mason back through the window, but she clearly noticed the aftermath of the food battle. While looking at her expression, I guessed that we wouldn't be having any more parties. I surmised that we wouldn't get to go home early either. I would have bet that we had one hell of a mess to clean up.

She stood at the doorway in deadly silence for a minute. Then she pointed her bony finger into the hallway. "Come now—all of you—every one of you little…." She must have bitten her tongue at that moment.

As we spilled out of the classroom one by one, and the food particles spilled off of each of us, I continued to hear her venting. "Heathens! Heathens—one and all!"

We began our march down the hallway toward the principal's office. About halfway there, Sister Theresa made a detour into the supply room. Like actors after a final dress rehearsal for a vaudeville show—thanks to the cupcake makeup—we waited for our director to critique our performance. Instead, she started passing out various cleaning supplies, and then she led us back to the devastated classroom.

When I walked back in the room, it looked a lot messier than I had initially thought. We were heathens. How did this happen? There was a little bit of vanilla icing on the American flag, and there was some chocolate smeared on the clock. We would need to use the ladder to get to both of those.

Sister Theresa laid it all on the line. "Not only will you not be going home early today, but if this room is not spick, as well as span, in a half an hour, there will be no Christmas break this year." If that wasn't enough, she added, "Every one of you will get a lump of coal for this." Then, she looked at her watch as she was leaving the room, and she closed the door behind her, which also had two cupcakes adorning it.

We looked around at each other for a brief moment, and not being quite sure what we were doing, twenty-eight little Catholic boys and girls moved like the dickens so that we could all be home caroling by Christmas eve. Nobody wanted to spend the holidays with Saint Luke. He probably wouldn't have been very generous to any of us.

By the time Sister Theresa made it back to the room, we had everything, including ourselves, about as clean as imaginable. Her stone face seemed to soften a little, but I still could not detect a smile. Then she announced, "Okay class, now open your textbooks to chapter four and start reading. I have to leave the room again, but I will be back immediately."

Moans and groans erupted throughout the classroom as we opened our books. Once again, luck was on my side. I noticed the friendly snowflakes that were waving to me from outside the window. Perhaps, Saint Luke was giving us his blessing. In no time at all, everything outside was covered in pure white. It would be a right

Christmas after all. Everyone else in the classroom had noticed the flakes too, and we instinctively closed our textbooks even before Sister Theresa returned to the classroom for one last announcement. It was inevitable.

As I walked through the hallway to leave for the day, I saw Sister Mary Catherine heading toward the principal's office. Just before she walked in the door, a piece of white paper dropped out of a stack that she was carrying, and it floated down to the floor. It reminded me of a large snowflake. I thought that it would be an opportunity for me to do at least one good deed before the holidays kicked in.

I picked up the paper and proceeded into the office. There weren't any souls in sight. I thought that I heard a noise in the back room. I didn't want to be in there too long, so I curiously walked back to take a peep. The door to the back room was shut. I took a quick glance through the glass door pane, and I noticed that Sister Mary Catherine and Sister Ann Margaret were embracing and kissing underneath what appeared to be a sprig of mistletoe. I moved swiftly out of view before they noticed me.

I determined that my good deed would have to go unrewarded. I dropped the paper onto Sister Ann Margaret's desk, and I decided to call it a day. Once again, I had witnessed a rare event. I pondered for a moment about what I saw. Then I figured that it was Christmas after all…and they are Sisters.

As I walked through the schoolyard, I noticed that the weather had warmed up just enough to turn it into a wet slushy snow that crunched under my feet with every step that I took. I didn't even make it half way across the yard before I saw the first snowball whizzing above my head. I ran for cover.

I headed for the alley, and I saw that Ratboy already had his ammunition lined up. They were more like ice balls than snowballs. He continued throwing them at various moving and stationary targets in the alley and around the schoolyard. I just stood there watching as he missed on every throw.

Then, I noticed that one of the younger kids was walking toward us. I remembered seeing him around the school, but I couldn't remember his name. He was probably in fourth or fifth grade. He seemed oblivious to everything around him. It sounded like he was singing.

As he got closer, I heard his innocent little voice sing out, the words to Jingle Bells. He either forgot the words, or he was thinking heavily about a Christmas wish because they just tapered off into nothing.

When Ratboy had the little kid clearly in his scope, he whispered, "Let's duck behind here so he won't see us."

I played along as the two of us hid behind an old, rotting picket fence. We waited in silence for the unsuspecting prey to walk past us. When he was about fifteen feet beyond where we were hiding, Ratboy sprung out into the alley and threw the rock hard ice ball at the little guy.

This time, Ratboy threw a perfect strike, and he jumped into the air in jubilation. It hit the little boy in the back of the head so hard that he collapsed to the ground! We stood there waiting for him to get back up…and waiting…and waiting…but he wouldn't get back up. He wasn't moving at all, not even the slightest quiver.

Ratboy suspended his celebration and just gawked at the small boy lying on top of the cold, white surface. We anxiously looked around to see if there were any witnesses. Not sure of what action to take, we ducked back behind the picket fence again to contemplate our next move.

Neither of us was talking about the assault, but I'm sure that Ratboy was at least as deep in thought as I was. Every so often we would take a peak in the alley. There was no sign of life. I guess that Ratboy figured that he had no choice but to pull out the half smoked joint from his torn, dirty coat pocket and smoke it while we waited out the tense circumstances that he put us in. It was another classic, ugly Ratboy situation, even uglier than usual. The suspense was killing me. I didn't do anything wrong, but I still felt guilty. At least I still had somewhat of a conscience left inside of me.

With a cavalier attitude, Ratboy lit the joint, took a couple tokes, and said, "Do you wanna hit?"

I just shook my head, which felt soaked from the combination of the snow flurries, the melting icicles that were dripping down on me from the overhang on the house above us, and by not wearing my new tassel cap that must have fallen out of my coat pocket somewhere between the school and the alley.

Ratboy looked like a wet varmint. It was a miserable situation that he got us into. He would easily soothe his own pain by hitting the joint while waiting for the boy to recover from the painful hit that he had delivered to him.

Before long, the marijuana scent became too enticing for me to ignore. Ratboy connected what was left of it to his roach clip. "Here, you can finish it." Then he pulled a ski mask out of his other coat pocket and covered his head completely with it. It made him look like a criminal.

By the time I finished smoking the joint, at least five minutes had passed since the last time either of us took a glance into the alleyway. We were hesitant to look again. We knew that if he was still lying there, it could be a real messy problem to deal with. As the sun finally started to appear from above the clouds, we decided to make an appearance from behind the fence.

As we walked into the alley, I kept my eyes firmly on Ratboy. I figured that his expression would tell the tale. Besides, it was his mess. When he was in full view of the crime scene, he quickly removed the ski mask from his head and just stared with his eyes wide open.

Still looking at him, I just said, "What?"

Slowly, I turned my head to look down the alley, and I saw that the little boy was gone. We walked over to where he had been lying, and we were able to make out the imprint of his little body in the snow. We looked all around, but there was no sight of anyone. I felt like I was hallucinating again as I gazed at the many footprints that were going in every possible direction. We couldn't tell which ones were his…if any?

Ratboy stared up into the sky in amazement. With the sun beaming down on his devilish face, he squinted and said, "The angels came down and took him away."

It sounded believable for a moment, but that was because I caught a good buzz from the reefer. The more I thought about it, the more idiotic Ratboy seemed. While he was still looking skyward, I bumped him with my shoulder. "Let's go dumb-ass."

As we continued walking down the alley, Ratboy asked, "What do you think we should do now?"

I just shook my head. "Nothing—not a thing."

There wasn't much that we could do. We didn't have many good options. We could have knocked on the nearby doors asking everyone if they knew the whereabouts of a small boy that Ratboy pulverized in the skull and left for dead. Hopefully, they wouldn't notice that we were high on dope. We could have notified the school of the incident, but that probably wouldn't have gone over too good either. We could have said something to our parents, but why ruin their holidays? By the time we reached the end of the alley, we decided to try to forget about it and just go on with the usual Merry fucking Christmas.

Chapter Twelve
Survivors

Nineteen Seventy-five was known as Holy Year. It was a special time that happened once every twenty-five years, at least that is what Sister Theresa told us in one of her propaganda-like speeches. It involved a pilgrimage to Rome or some other equivalent event, and it was also a unique opportunity for the remission of sins. She said that we should be thankful to be at Saint Luke during this Great Jubilee. I didn't care much about that stuff. We weren't going on a field trip to Italy either, and after her initial uninspiring speech we didn't hear much else about Holy Year.

In January we were focused mostly on sports, but not so much on our basketball team. We had again slipped into mediocrity. I didn't care about that anymore either. I was still stuck at one point for the season. I didn't get many chances to walk onto the game floor. However, I did have a nice opportunity for my fingers do some traveling under Cathy's skirt on the back of the bus coming from an away game against Saint Jude.

The sport that we were all focused on was football. No, we didn't have a team at Saint Luke, but we were all excited when we discovered that the Steel team was making their first foray into the final, super championship game. Nobody was shooting hoops in the yard in January, but there were several foam footballs whizzing overhead at any given time.

Everyone pretended that they were Swann or Franco or Mean Joe. Even the nuns got into the act. Sister Mary Catherine who looked like she could play linebacker would sometimes mention the Immaculate Reception during one of her lectures…or was it…Conception? She had to be a fan regardless of the mix up.

It was a good thing that we had something to look forward to. Everything else seemed rather dreary after the holidays were over with. We still had about five months left to the school year, and it was always possible that one of us wouldn't make it that far. I thought about that as I tossed Ratboy a pass to the far end of the schoolyard. Some of us lived in a more dangerous world than others did.

When I saw Ratboy complete the pass, I was about to applaud. It was the first time that he didn't drop the ball, but my attention was quickly diverted when I saw a familiar face coming toward me. I was pretty certain that it was the kid that Ratboy clobbered with the snowball a few weeks earlier. He was bundled up with a hat and scarf. As he got closer, I was sure that it was him.

I approached the lad and tried to ask, "Aren't you the kid that…uh…?"

Without knowing what I was asking, he just shook his head timidly as if not to appear guilty of something. I didn't know what to say. He seemed like a nice kid. I just uttered, "Hi, I'm Tom. What's your name?"

With a sad expression on his face and a stutter to his voice, he returned, "I'm St—St—Steven." Then he walked away slowly and awkwardly toward the school.

I looked over at Ratboy, who was pointing at me and laughing. I thought that if he hit the poor kid so hard with the snowball that it made him permanently stupid, I would not forgive him. Least of all, I didn't think that it was so funny.

On the other hand, Ratboy had been hit on the noggin so many times in his life that I should feel sorry for him. With all the knocks he took—along with the pot smoking, his brain was probably going in reverse.

Because he still had a stupid grin on his face, I yelled, "Go long, Chuck!" I kept waving my hand at him to go even further while yelling, "Deep! Go deep!"

I threw the ball as far as I could because I knew that Ratboy would try to fetch it. As he ran for it, he slipped on the slick surface and fell hard to the ground. It was enough to get rid of the stupid grin on his face, and it was partial payback for the snowball incident. Of course, Ratboy was used to the pain, but little Steven probably wasn't.

Ratboy was still lying on the ground like he was injured. I walked over to see if he was putting on an act. I noticed that his eyes were completely closed. I started kicking him in the stomach, and then he slowly opened his eyes and said, "Back from the dead, huh?" The stupid grin reappeared.

It gave me reassurance about something that I had been suspecting, something that Uncle Joe had mentioned before, and something that my parents had warned me about several times in the past: Ratboy would never amount to anything, but for the time being, he was a survivor, as was little Steven and myself. Still, it was only January, and June was still a long way off. Sister Theresa told us that anything could happen in Holy Year, and we would have to learn to accept whatever circumstances that we are graced with.

On a cold and dismal Monday—the day after the Steel team won the big game, Sister Ann Margaret gave instructions for all of the teachers to tell us that we would have a special assembly in the gymnasium at ten o'clock. Some of us thought that it would be a victory celebration; others whispered something about Holy Year.

When we were all comfortably seated in our chairs, Sister Ann Margaret walked up to the podium and grasped a microphone. "For those of you that haven't heard, there was a terrible accident this weekend. One of our sixth graders here at Saint Luke—Arnold Weyner was drowned while playing near the river."

I looked around at all of the surprised and worrisome faces that filled the makeshift auditorium. I don't think that anyone expected such an announcement. The name sounded familiar to me, and I tried to picture his happy, little face. I recalled feeling the same uneasiness a few years earlier when I found out that Clemente—my greatest sports hero was killed in a plane crash.

Then, Sister Ann Margaret announced, "We will now proceed to the church for a special mass. Afterwards, you will return to your normal classes. Father Spencer and I will visit each classroom this afternoon to talk with you."

With the exception of getting out of doing our regular assignments that morning, it was a gloomy day. The sun had refused to make an appearance as we walked back and forth from the school to the church. Most of the kids were quiet. A few of them felt bad enough to shed tears.

Some of the kids weren't taking it so bad though. I saw Ratboy eyeing up the poor box when we walked into the church. He didn't want to break with precedence. It had become another addiction for him.

Then, on the way back to the school, I saw Marty making obscene, drowning gestures to some of the other kids. He held his nose like he was going under. Then he flailed his arms and cried out, "Help me! Help me!" I tried to ignore him, and then I thought—yea, you're drowning alright, pal.

I found out later on that Arnold tried to walk over the frozen Corliss Creek—a feat that Ratboy and I had achieved at least twice in the past. Apparently, the creek wasn't frozen enough, and when he got about halfway across, there was a big crack. One of his friends stood there in shock while watching from the shore as Arnold dropped below the ice. Because of the slow response, he was under the frigid water for at least an hour.

My great grandfather died about a year earlier, but he was about ninety-eight and a half years old. I didn't think that it was supposed to happen to little kids. Sister Ann Margaret told us that God had given Arnold an invitation to come visit him. I just hoped that I wouldn't get one anytime soon. I wasn't ready for it, and the way things were going for me, I may never be ready for that death trip.

Father Spencer let Ratboy work the funeral mass. I was glad that he didn't ask me. Ten bucks or no money, I didn't want to be anywhere near Arnold's casket. I was becoming unenthusiastic about even being in the church. I wondered what I needed to do to resign from the altar boy position. Holy Year or not, I thought that I had been punished enough.

A few weeks after Arnold's demise, Sister Ann Margaret made another announcement just in front of the eighth grade class. We sat there in quiet anticipation. We wondered what other bad news she would spring on us. When she was sure that she garnered everyone's attention, she announced, "Starting this week we have a new student here at Saint Luke. His name is Louis Selmon. His family moved here from Chicago. I would like everyone to treat him with the utmost respect."

I wondered why she chose the words utmost respect. What was he supposed to be—a prince or something? Was she afraid that if we didn't act respectfully, his family would move back to Chicago and the school would lose another deposit? Perhaps they could no longer get enough students from the local gene pool, so they needed to campaign outside the area. Maybe they needed to extradite children from other areas of the country in order to keep the seats filled.

As I walked into my first period class the next morning, there was an extremely unfamiliar person sitting at one of the desks in the last row. He was unlike anyone I had ever seen at Saint Luke. He was colored. I wondered what Uncle Joe meant when I overheard him say to one of the nuns the other day, "I hope they don't make fun of his afro." I didn't think that they were allowed to be Catholic. I wondered how they finagled it. God knows they needed the tuition, especially after they lost a couple more years of fees from the Weyner family. I wondered how good the new kid could play basketball.

Later in the week, we had unseasonably warm weather for the end of January. The snow had melted on the schoolyard, and we thought that we would try to negotiate some hoops during lunch period. I was playing Twenty One with the Santino brothers, and I noticed that Louis Selmon was walking toward us.

Mike dribbled the ball at the foul line. When he saw Louis, he bounced the ball toward him and asked, "Would you like to play with us, new kid?"

Louis let the ball bounce past him, and then he said in a mature, intelligent voice, "No thanks, I don't play basketball."

He continued walking toward the back of the yard where he found a dry spot to rest on. We suspended play of the game as we continued to examine him. He pulled out a paperback book from his coat pocket and began to read it. I thought about how he just killed a few of the old biased theories that I was taught over the years. No to basketball—yes to a book?

The only other colored kids that I knew of lived in the projects. They either attended the public school, or they didn't go to any school. Louis didn't look like them. He didn't talk, nor did he walk like them either. I would have bet that every one of those black is beautiful—a mind is a terrible thing (to waste) project kids could play basketball better than they could read.

I was only half focused on playing hoops because I kept looking over at Louis. I must have been impressed with him. He didn't seem to be intimidated by any of us. He seemed to be above it. I think that he knew what it meant to be a survivor too.

I kept wondering what he was reading. Who reads books anyway, unless it was an assignment or something? Occasionally, I would go into the school's library and read a book on sports statistics, or maybe one of the classics like Curious George, The Five Chinese Brothers, or one of the Dr. Seuss stories, but Louis appeared to be reading a book—book.

Most of the other kids in the yard were examining him too. Then Mike said, "Why's that duda-bayba reading a book for? He'll never be as smart as me."

I felt like telling Mike that the duda-bayba was probably already smarter than he would ever be, and that it could have been predetermined from birth. Louis may not have been a genius, but Mike wasn't smarter than anyone, except for maybe…Ratboy. I didn't know a lot about anything, but some things were easy to figure out. Mike, along with some of the other misfits at Saint Luke may have survived so far, but the road ahead could be a perilous one for them.

Toward the end of lunch period, Louis closed the book and stuffed it back into his coat pocket. He walked past us again on his way back into the school. There was a basketball lying off to the side of the court. He picked up the ball and dribbled it a few times, and with one hand, he threw it about thirty-feet to make a perfect swish. Then, he turned back toward the school like it was no big deal.

With an amazed expression, Mike yelled, "I thought you said you didn't play?"

Louis turned back toward him for a moment. "That's right. I don't play."

I stood there thinking…where the heck did this kid come from? Then I remembered—Chicago. I didn't have the nerve to look down on him. Sister Ann Margaret would have been happy to know that he did in fact have my utmost respect. It wasn't immediate, but he garnered it rather quickly.

After all, I couldn't imagine him streaking through the schoolyard…vandalizing the school…robbing the church…or smoking dope. Perhaps he was sent here from the almighty for some purpose after Arnold was taken away. There would always be mysteries of the faith that none of us could quite comprehend.

Later in the afternoon, Sister Mary Catherine got us to play the juvenile what do you want to be when you become an adult game. When we were finished, there were three answers that stood out in my mind, including the one that I submitted.

I replied, "I want to be a mailman." I just couldn't think of anything more interesting to say. I remembered seeing the postman driving past me on my way to school, and I thought it was a cool looking vehicle. It reminded me of an army jeep, even though the steering wheel was on the wrong side.

My level of respect for Louis dropped slightly when he had the gall to say, "I want to be president." Could you imagine such a thing? He got a few jeers from some of his classmates. He may have been reaching too high, or maybe his parents were making him jump, but not enough to want to play basketball. He did mention that his dad was president of his company.

The best and possibly most believable response — depending how you look at it — came from Ratboy. When it was his turn, with his typical dazed and confused expression, he answered,

"I want to be a spaceman."

I don't know if anyone of us were looking that far ahead. I think that we mostly wanted to survive our last few months at Saint Luke. Then we could move on to our next adventure whether on land, water, or in space.

Chapter Thirteen
Changing of the Guard

On February Second, in a small town about eighty miles north of us, a few hundred assholes gathered in the early morning freeze to let a little rodent try to predict their future. It didn't mean shit according to my grandfather. It was probably as accurate as Ratboy trying to predict the weather forecast for the next six weeks at Saint Luke.

The next morning, I realized that there was another shadow that I hadn't seen in a while—the one that belonged to Father Leonard Spencer. I was glad that I wasn't summoned for altar boy service for a few weeks. I hadn't seen the Batmobile parked in its usual spot in a while. I did remember seeing a police car parked there about a week earlier though.

Father Murphy had secretly become the new pastor. There weren't any big announcements—just a brief notice in the church bulletin mentioning that Spencer transferred to a diocese in the Boston, Massachusetts area. Since Murphy had to fill Spencer's shoes, they decided to hire another pervert…oops, I mean—another priest to take over Murphy's soft position.

I thought that it might be a good time for me to finally retire from altar boy service. A few other eighth graders had already quit.

Even Ratboy concluded that he probably wouldn't have the same barter system with Murphy. Besides, we would be graduating in a few months so Murphy would be doing himself a favor by recruiting some of the younger kids for the long term. Ratboy, and I had too many skeletons. We were dedicated sinners.

Father Murphy set up a meeting after school the following Monday with all of us future men of the cloth to discuss current and future events. I figured that it was as good a time as any to give him my resignation. I just wasn't the good little Catholic boy that he was hoping for, and neither was Ratboy or Tony for that matter, but the three of us showed up anyway. I didn't have Murphy quite figured out yet. I thought that I would at least give him the courtesy to hear what he had to say.

There were several other altar boys at the meeting. Some of them had already worked with Murphy when he presided over the mass. Most of them were in fifth, sixth or seventh grade, with the exception of Calvin Gregory who joined up about a month after Ratboy and I got lured in. Most of them seemed rather…holy? The youngest ones looked like the prototype Catholic altar boy…at least for the time being. I was sure that some of them would grow wiser later on. They hadn't been around long enough yet.

I thought that I would give Father Murphy an opportunity to give us his penance. Then I would break the news to him. I sat there listening while trying to decide how I would tell him. He didn't have a big speech prepared. He didn't mention anything about Spencer. I imagined he had at least a shovelful of dirt on him, but that he preferred to keep it buried.

He had a kind, magnetic face—totally opposite of Spencer. His expressions made up for the lack of words. After mentioning a few things about himself and the church, he just looked at us and said, "I'm counting on all of you guys to help me turn Holy Year into the best year ever at Saint Luke."

As soon as I heard that, I knew that I wouldn't be hanging up my cassock after all. He seemed like a smart man. He looked humble—sympathetic, and we all seemed to share that sympathy with him. He played the Holy Year card well. He didn't have to say a lot, but he knew how to get his point across. We all just sat there nodding our heads like devoted disciples. The young kids were already brainwashed, and I even felt like I was under hypnosis.

As we were leaving, Father Murphy turned to Ratboy. "Mr. Dalton, I need you to come with me to the rectory please."

I hung around to watch the two of them leave the school building, stroll down the walkway, and right into the damned rectory. I wasn't sure what it was all about, and, quite frankly, I didn't care to know…well, maybe I cared a little, especially if it had to do with money or the Spencer situation.

As I was leaving the school, I spotted my wannabe girlfriend hanging around the schoolyard. Once again, I couldn't resist playing the game.

"What are you up to, Cathy?"

"Five foot-three…the last time I checked."

"What? No, I mean…why are you hanging around here?"

"We are supposed to get together for cheerleader practice at four o'clock."

"Outside? Now?"

"Yea, I'm waiting for Jean and Veronica."

That didn't sound quite right. I didn't see any other girls around. It was freezing out, and the basketball season was almost over. She was clever and a good liar. Her game was at least as good as mine was. While we were trying to figure each other out, I asked, "Do you want to walk around the school until they get here?"

She glanced at her watch. I noticed that it was already a few minutes after four o'clock. "Sure…why not?"

After making a few circles around Saint Luke, we ended up in front of the gym entrance. I tried to determine what our next move should be. Then I made a quick shiver motion while pointing at the door. I noticed that it was unlocked. We decided to make our way inside.

The lights were out, and there wasn't an authority figure or anyone else around. We walked across the gym floor, and up the steps to the stage area—a good place for any performance. The curtain was closed, and we went around the side to get behind it. I noticed that the grand piano was sitting in the corner, and it had some old, ragged blankets that covered it all the way down to the floor. I kept staring at it while wondering about my artistic ability.

The old piano didn't get much use. I thought that it was a shame to waste such an expensive instrument. I didn't have any musical talent, but I still considered myself to be creative. It looked like an invitation of some sort. I pondered about the possibilities.

I was happy about the position that I was in, especially because it was my idea for once. I took control of the situation, and Cathy went along with it, instead of the other way around. I was excited again. I knew that I was going to sin again. I didn't care. I wasn't even concerned if I got caught. Then, as I felt a heavy dose of adrenaline running through my body, I grabbed her hand and led her underneath the piano like two kids playing some funky version of hide-and-go-seek.

We sat there for a minute in the dark while not saying anything. Then I felt her warm, moist breath on my face. The kissing and hugging came next. Before long, we had totally stripped down, our clothes beneath us. I felt that it could be the greatest moment of my history at Saint Luke. I always wanted to score big inside the gym before my time was up.

Cathy instinctively stretched out with her back on the ground. I felt that it was an invitation for me to be on top. After more kissing and fondling, she grabbed hold of my little rascal and moved it toward an area of a most wonderful warmth. I felt like she was trying to guide me inside of her. Could this be it? I wondered.

The problem was that I couldn't get it to go in. It stayed soft for some reason. I started to feel numb all over my body. Cathy started to stroke it, but it didn't seem to help any. I tried to focus on something to help the situation, but I kept thinking about Captain Kangaroo for some reason. Then I wondered how large of a penis Mr. Green Jeans had. That didn't seem to help either.

After several attempts, Cathy whispered, "What do we do about this here? Huh? What do we do?" She kept playing with it like if it was a little rubber toy.

I didn't say a word. When she stopped toying with it, I started rubbing my genitals on hers. I started to make small circling motions, and then large circling motions. It felt more like a game—a feel good game. I was never able to make it inside of her little cave, but I think that it still counted as being sex. I kept doing the circle jerk for about a half hour until I was exhausted and dripping in sweat. I hoped that something else would drip…or shoot out of me, but it never happened.

We just lay there for a minute to catch our breath. Then, it just started to feel weird that we were naked underneath a piano on a stage inside of a darkened gymnasium. I looked at Cathy, and barely able to see her I said, "Let's get out of here."

I felt that it was a good experience, but it wasn't as great of a moment as I was striving for. It seemed to be a little more dubious and a little less than legendary. I still felt the pleasure of a big smile on my face which was immediately followed by the pain of a large crack down the middle of my wintry chapped lip. I was beginning to learn the many ways that pain and pleasure can complement each other.

Then, like a fool, I tried to stand up while momentarily forgetting the low ceiling that the piano provided. I smacked my skull, and I thought that I heard a note ring out. While I was dressing, I started thinking of a few tunes that might have used that particular note—more pain and pleasure.

We starting walking through the gym, and I realized once again that I got away with another dirty little deed. My good luck continued. I thought that perhaps Saint Luke wasn't such a bad place, and that Holy Year wasn't a bad thing at all. It was possible that I might even miss the school someday.

When we made it back outside, I said, "I guess that you aren't having practice today then?"

She smiled. "Uh…maybe it's tomorrow."

As we parted I thought that tomorrow sounded like another invitation. We were never officially boyfriend-girlfriend. There were no proposals…no agreements…no proclamations. It was just a thing…or maybe a fling. It certainly wouldn't be announced in the church bulletin, but, just like Father Spencer, I needed to have my dirty little secrets too.

I started walking away from the school, and then I heard a voice yell, "Tom—wait up!" I kept walking until I heard, "Dopeboy—wait up!"

I looked back, and I saw Ratboy running toward me. I wondered if he was in the rectory the whole time that I was dancing on stage with Cathy. Going from her to Ratboy was the equivalent of having a diamond ring on my finger, and then a moment later the ring was gone and a booger took its place. He had a lot of nerve calling me Dopeboy. He was the dopiest guy around in more ways than one. Telling him to not be an idiot was like telling Uncle Joe or some of the nuns to not be sadistic, or telling certain priests to not be perverted. Spencer may have had both illnesses.

When Ratboy caught up to me, he asked, "What are you up to?"

I instinctively responded, "Five foot-six…the last time I checked."

"What? What do you mean?"

His confused expression told me that he didn't get it. I didn't want to tell him anything about my recent experience, so I said, "Nothing—just hanging around."

Then it was my turn. I asked suspiciously, "What are you up to?"

He shook his head and said, "Nothing."

I could see that it was one of those nothing conversations that was going nowhere. I'm sure that each of us had something interesting to say, but neither of us wanted to sing. I continued the dialogue anyway. "What are you gonna do now, Chuck?"

"Nothing. How about you?"

"Not a damn thing."

As we kept walking, I realized that I had the upper hand. Ratboy had no idea that I was inside of the gym with Cathy, but I knew exactly where he was and who he was with. At first I pretended like I didn't care, but then it started eating me up. "So, what were you doing in the rectory with Father Murphy?"

"Nothing—just mostly talking about…uh…."

"What happened with Spencer?"

Ratboy just shook his head and looked away from me. My instincts told me that his conversation with Murphy was mostly based on him keeping mum about the dirty Spencer situation. I didn't ask him anymore questions about it. It was his problem to deal with, and I didn't want to make it mine.

We walked past the spot where Spencer used to park his shiny, black Cadillac, and we saw that there was a dull, gray Buick parked there instead. I asked Ratboy, "Is that Murphy's car?"

"Yea, I think it is."

I just shook my head while thinking that Father Murphy had only been with Saint Luke for about two years, and he would probably have to put in a few more years of service to work his way up to owning a nice luxury car, but who knows, perhaps he was one of those truly humble servants that we used to hear about.

It felt as if an era was truly coming to an end. I thought that maybe the true purpose of Holy Year was for the school to go through a cleansing period. They got rid of Spencer, and pretty soon they would rid themselves of a whole mess of little Catholic sinners. Maybe, little Arnold Weyner was sacrificed as a way for all of us to pay for our evil deeds. Maybe, Brother Louis Selmon was sent here to lead us to the Promised Land. Maybe, my imagination was too vivid for my own good, and none of it meant anything.

I looked at Ratboy and wondered what he was thinking. He was probably contemplating where he could steal his next dollar, and when he could score some more pot. I, on the other hand, kept thinking about having more sex with Cathy…and maybe some of the other girls in my class…and maybe some of the seventh graders…and maybe even one of the nuns, particularly a youthful, awkward looking, Sister Deloris, a recent addition to the flock. We were told to welcome her with open hearts and minds. I had fantasized about welcoming her by opening something else. After all, it was Holy Year, and I often thought that I should give something back to the school.

Chapter Fourteen

Falling

The winter snow was melting away, and before long we were into March—a traditional month at Saint Luke. We completed our basketball season a few weeks earlier, and it was time for our annual awards banquet.

We didn't win any of our tournaments. We lost as many games as we won. We wouldn't be adding anything to that fabulous trophy case, but the school still decided to spring for miniature trophies to give everyone on the team for our fine efforts.

I had no complaints. I got to play for five minutes in the last game of the year. I scored a lay-up, and it brought my season total to three points. It was the only two-pointer that I ever made in a game. It would also be the first and last trophy that I would receive.

They would serve us roast beef, crunchy salad, and peach pie. We felt like kings for a couple hours. It was a rare moment of Saint Luke's generosity. There still must have been an angle somewhere. It was almost too good of an evening. I was waiting for someone to spoil it.

Toward the end of the ceremony, Mike Santino felt that he needed to play one last gag on one of the other players. His biggest target all year was Stanley Howard who just happened to be seated between Mike and lucky old me.

When Stanley stood up to reach for something across the table, I saw Mike pull his chair back about two feet. Once again, I just went along with it, not wanting to spoil the moment for him. Mike sat there grinning until Stanley proceeded to settle back into his seat. I could see that it was a disaster in process.

It looked like Stanley was moving in slow motion. When he got to the point where his butt should have been in contact with the wood of the chair, a frightened expression drew across his face, and he started to lose his balance. It reminded me of a scary Hitchcock film.

As Stanley fell hard to the floor, and smacked his head even harder on the front of the chair, Mike, the jerk responded with, "Oh my god! Are you alright, Stanley? How did that happen?"

Looking a bit dazed, Stanley looked at Mike and asked, "What did you do that for?"

With an angry tone, Mike returned, "What are you talking about? I didn't do anything to you." Then he tried to pass the blame along by looking toward me.

Stanley gave me a dirty look, as if he thought that I was the guilty party. He looked like he was in pain, and I noticed that his left arm was severely scraped up. He had to know from past experiences that Mike was the perpetrator—not me, but he just sat there sulking and occasionally looking at me with a puzzled expression.

As the evening was wrapping up, I saw Mike pull Stanley over to the other side of the auditorium. It appeared that they were into some heavy dialogue. Every so often they would take a glance over toward me. I could tell that Mike had another scheme in development. I just wanted to get the hell out of there with my little trophy before it got broken.

Just before I made it to the door, I heard Mike yell, "Tom! Tom, wait a minute! Hold up!"

I looked back and saw that he was motioning with his hand for me to wait. I gestured back to him with my finger pointing toward the door to let him know that I had to leave, but I still waited for him anyway.

He hurried over toward me while Stanley stayed put. "Tom—good news, you and Stanley are going to fight after the banquet."

"What for? Why would I fight him?" Good news for whom, I wondered?

"He thinks that you pulled his chair. You have to fight him. You can't get out of it now."

"But, I didn't pull his chair. You…I mean…someone…else must have pulled it."

Even though just about everyone in the auditorium, including Stanley, had to know that Mike was the culprit, I was afraid to tell him to his face that I knew he was the one that pulled Stanley's chair.

I looked over at Stanley. He had an expression on his face that was probably similar to mine. It said that he didn't want to fight me either, but Mike insisted on it. At that moment—more than any other time, I wished that I had the nerve to smack Mike in the mouth, but I didn't even have the nerve to hit Stanley, so I certainly wouldn't be hitting Santino.

"Oh…I don't know, Mike. I don't want to get into trouble," I reasoned.

"You won't. We'll wait till everyone leaves, and we'll go up to the alley afterwards."

I started visualizing the dreaded alley scene, and I realized that in eight years I never had an official fight. I had a brief scuffle when I was in sixth grade with a kid named Benny Worms, but we mostly just shoved each other back and forth. Then we finished the fight by spitting in each other's faces. There were a few occasions in the past when I smacked Ratboy around for the fun of it just like everyone else did, but nothing for the record books. Cathy beat me up once when we were in sixth grade. She finished me off with a firm set of noogies. I thanked all of the saints that there were no witnesses for that one. Our fondness for each other grew from there.

I had hoped that the three points I scored on the court and the many points I scored with Cathy—which eventually got leaked out to everyone—were enough for me to secure my legacy at Saint Luke, but apparently not. I still needed to raise my status level.

I didn't know what to say. Mike kept waiting for an answer.

"Uh…yea…okay. I'll do it, I guess."

"Don't worry, Tom, you can kick his ass easily—no problem."

Then he went over to talk to Stanley again, probably to tell him not to worry because he could easily kick my ass too. I walked out the door and headed for the alleyway. I hoped that Stanley would chicken out, and I really hoped that Mike would find something else to do with himself.

I stood alone in the alley to await my fate. The sky was overcast. The gravel surface was dirty and wet. With the exception of the shiny trophy that I set on the ground, everything else around me looked…unappealing.

After a few minutes, I spotted Mike and Stanley walking toward me. It looked like Mike was coaching him along the way. I thought that maybe I should start running home, but how could I? Besides, if I chickened out, it would only fuel Stanley's confidence, and Mike's anger for the next time. I felt weak, and my heart palpitated. As they got closer, I knew that it was too late to get out of it.

So, there we were—me and Stanley—just staring each other down and not saying a word, and there was Mike with his arms folded and using facial expressions to prompt both of us into action. He was one part coach, one part referee, and many parts jag-off.

When I gazed at Stanley, he looked like he wanted to tell me that he didn't want to be in this awful situation any more than I did. When I looked at Mike, his eyes told me that he already rang the bell for the first round, and if he didn't see some action pretty quick, he might have to get physical himself.

Still not being sure of how I wanted to handle it, I did come to the conclusion that I would rather take my chances getting a beating from Stanley than a more severe one from Mike. I also decided to initiate the first action, which, as usual, was a simple shove.

Stanley waited a moment, looked at Mike who nodded, and then he pushed me back. Hoping that it would be just another boring match of shoves, I gave him another, and, once again, he returned one of his. We went back and forth about six or seven times. Then I heard Mike grunt with dissatisfaction.

I figured that I had to increase the violence level somewhat, so I charged toward my opponent. He moved to the left, and I got tripped up all the way to the ground. I grabbed him around his legs and brought him down to the asphalt to join me. Then it became a game of amateur wrestling holds.

We rolled around on the ground while each of us made weak attempts to choke each other into submission. There were no punches thrown, and no blood was spilled. We were basically just wearing ourselves out while trying to please *Don* Santino.

The pace slowed to the point where we had one another in what each of us assumed would be a match ending death grip. He had my right arm pinned behind my back while his left hand was around my neck. I applied the scissors with my legs around his abdomen while my left hand pulled at his crotch. It was ridiculous. I felt like an idiot.

Mike must have been bored with the whole spectacle when I heard him say, "I'll see you two fools later. Good luck!"

Stanley and I just looked at each other on the ground. I wondered if my face was as blue as his was purple. We knew that we were fools. We gradually started loosening our holds on each other. A sense of relief came over his face, and I felt the same on mine. Mike was already near the end of the alley and he wasn't looking back. There was nobody else around. So we started to get up. I was often lucky not to have anyone witness the more awkward situations in my life.

Stanley and I didn't say a word to each other. We walked over to the side of the alley where the trophy that I had received from the banquet sat on the ground next to the one that he got. It became so ironic. Neither of us did much during the basketball season to earn the prestigious award. It was as if Mike arranged the fight to make Stanley and me worthy of receiving the same prize that he was given for all of his hard work on the court. When I reached for my prize, in an odd way it did feel like it was a little more earned.

In one sense, I was glad that I had the altercation with Stanley as a way to help build up my confidence. On the other side of my brain, I thought that he was an okay fella, and I was a little bit concerned of how he would perceive me in the future. We would probably never be friends after our fight, but, once again, it wasn't my fault. It was all Mike's doing.

The second big March event was our Saint Patrick's Day Pageant. This was always of great importance to the school, and other than the basketball games, it was the biggest event that Saint Luke sold tickets to any willing spectators. They decided to raise the admission price from the previous year. It was probably to make up for the generous basketball banquet they gave us.

They had a pretty good racket going. With a town that was full of Flanagan's, O'Malley's, and McDermott's, they couldn't miss. There were a lot of little greenhorns in the school that were happy to take part in the festivities. Of course, the school made sure that everyone of us got involved in one aspect or another. It wasn't quite as ridiculous as Ground Hog Day, but I still didn't want to wear the color. I didn't want to completely destroy my image.

Even though it was a foolish tradition, I have to admit that I enjoyed the lyrics to some of the songs. I had every one of the tunes memorized from repetition over the years. It was the only time of the year that I would set aside my beloved top 40 hits that were usually floating around in my head. We were able to act some of the songs out on stage.

When I sang "My Wild Irish Rose", I felt it in the pit of my stomach. During the first half of the song, a romantic feeling tingled through my body, but by the song's climax, another feeling overcame me, and I just wanted to drag that wild, part Irish girl—Cathy back under the piano to do the jig again.

We acted like a bunch of clowns during the chorus of "Too Ra Loo Ra Loo Ral". Then, when I sang "Harrigan", a rare bout of rowdiness tempted me to beat the crap out of Ratboy for turning me on to another kind of green clover. On the night of March Seventeenth, we had a packed house. That's because Saint Luke decided to add cheap, beer onto the refreshment list for the first time. It was another ploy to help offset the drop in tuition that they had experienced the past few years, or to help pay for that damned generous banquet.

The performance went fairly well over all, with the exception of Ratboy splitting his pants on stage while trying to do a crazy stunt. In another school production earlier in the year, he was given the *biggest* role in the play—an oak tree.

Then, just as the show was coming to a close and the curtain was dropping, I heard a ruckus coming from the back of the auditorium. There was some pushing and shoving going on from some of the adults. Later on I heard that it was because they ran out of the piss green beer.

The next major event was the school dance. It was something that they started just a year earlier, and it was exclusively for seventh and eighth graders. I didn't get to go the previous year because I came down with the chickenpox. I wasn't that excited about going, but I didn't want to *chicken* out on my final year.

Sister Ann Margaret told all of us fine Christian gentlemen that we should ask one the young ladies to accompany us, and, of course, to be on our best behavior. I didn't ask Cathy or any other girl to go with me. As far as I know, I don't think that any of the other gentleman asked anyone of the ladies either. As far as the best behavior…well….

The dance was scheduled to begin on Friday night at six o'clock. Ratboy asked me to meet him on the Layers at five. I wore the newest outfit that I got from Sonny's Sport Shop: a red imitation silk shirt, shiny black slacks, and of course — the platform shoes.

Sister Ann Margaret didn't mention anything about a dress code, so I wasn't surprised to see Ratboy approach me wearing a torn jeans jacket and a wrinkled T-shirt that had a design of a glittery reefer plant on it. Maybe he just wanted to be noticed, but from my point of view he stuck out like a sore…body?

When I first noticed the design, I just shook my head, and he said, "What? What's wrong?" He just didn't get it, and it was possible that he wouldn't get into the dance either.

As I pointed at his T-shirt, he reached into his jacket and pulled out a bottle that was about two thirds filled. I looked at the label which read Mad Dog 20/20.

Ratboy took a swig and then handed it to me. "Here, man— this is really good stuff. Take a swig."

How could I resist? I grasped the bottle and wiped Ratboy's slobber from the mouth of it. I took a quick taste, which put a sour expression on my face. I imagined what piss would taste like. I thought about what the green beer might have tasted like. I remembered what the mouthwash tasted like. Any one of those liquids could have been an improvement over the cheap wine. I took a few more swallows anyway, and I felt the effects quickly settling inside me. It was a lot stronger than the altar wine.

Ratboy smiled with his crooked teeth. "Good, huh?"

"Yea, real good! Where did you get it?"

"I swiped it from uh…."

I just nodded my head. I didn't ask him who he stole it from because some of the evidence was already inside of me. We just kept taking turns until the bottle bottomed out. My buzz had gotten a lot more...buzzed by then.

Ratboy tossed the empty bottle at a telephone pole, and I watched it shatter into a million pieces. Then he started laughing loudly — too loudly. It hurt my ears. He reminded me of the devil. The devil that would accompany me to the dance!

Ratboy yelled, "Let's go!" Then we headed down the Layers and toward the school.

When we got in front of the hippie house, Ratboy grabbed my shoulder. "Hold it! I need to make a stop here." He opened the gate, and then looked back at me and asked, "Are you coming in or not?"

No, would have been the intelligent answer, but I wasn't so full of smarts anymore. I followed him up to the porch. Ratboy rapped on the door a few times. When there was no quick response, he twisted the knob and pushed open the door. Then I was standing inside of the last place that I would ever want to be.

The light was dim, but I could see enough to notice how dusty and poorly kept everything looked. I saw cobwebs everywhere. I thought I saw a spider crawling its way down an old wooden banister that circled all the way up to the top floor.

I heard music coming from another room...somewhere? I didn't recognize it, and it had a spooky sound to it. A chilling effect came over me. Ratboy started moving toward the melody. I just stood frozen with my back up to the door and my hand comfortably resting on the greasy knob.

Ratboy looked back at me and whispered, "Come on, Tom. It's okay."

I just shook my head and allowed him to go it alone. I stood there watching him until he was completely out of my view. Then the music stopped, and I could barely hear voices. I kept looking around for a ghost to appear. The wall to the side of me had something written on it, but I could barely make it out. Hell something? Helter Skeleton? I kept trying to read it.

Several minutes passed by, and then I noticed a shadow moving from the top of the stairwell. I heard faint footsteps. I started breathing heavier while noticing the strong smell of the hobo wine with every one of my exhales. It felt like someone was staring at me, and it made my skin itch.

I tried to turn the knob, but I somehow pulled it out of the door. I must have broken it! I looked around nervously. Then I stuck the knob back into the opening and tried to do a quick fix. It was loose, and I couldn't get it to work. I kept jiggling it back and forth until I finally heard a click. As I started to open the door, I felt someone's hand grab my shoulder. I felt my asshole pucker up, and I nearly jumped out of my shoes. I turned around, and I saw that it was Ratboy — thank God!

As soon as we got out on the porch, Ratboy started rolling a joint, and then he moistened it with his sloppy, wet tongue. After he smoked it about halfway down, he tried to pass it to me. This time I turned him down. I already had plenty of poison in my system from the bad wine.

I stood there with him until he polished off the doobie. Then I asked, "Are you ready to go to the dance yet?"

He shook his head. "I'm not going to the dance, man."

"What? Why did you change your mind?"

"I was never going. That shit is for nerds."

I wasn't angry at him. At that point, I wasn't sure if I wanted to go either, but I thought that I would give it a shot anyway. "Okay Chuck, I'll catch you later then."

I started walking away, and for some reason, Chuck went back into the house. It must have been his ultimate destination, and I was still trying to get to mine. I felt totally out of sorts. I tried to remember the lyrics to "Too Ra Loo Ra Loo Ral", but I kept screwing it up. I had to face the fact that I was at least half drunk while attempting to make an appearance at a proper Catholic school dance.

It had to be at least six o'clock, and most of the kids would be there already. A few of the nuns would also be there to keep an eye on everyone. I started worrying about getting shaken down at the door. I started to tremble in fear. It wasn't the same type of fear that I felt in the hippie house—the fear of death! It was more like the fear of embarrassment, or the fear of getting scolded, or even the fear of being laughed at.

When I got close to my destination, I stood about one hundred feet from the entrance—off to the side of the building. I tried to build up my courage while occasionally taking a peak at the entrance door. I saw a few kids go inside, and they seemed to be laughing and having fun. I wasn't laughing. Deep down in my gut, I knew that I wanted to dance. I felt that I made a big mistake, and the misery started to kick in.

I didn't think that I could do it, so I started to walk away. I was about halfway home, and then I turned around and headed back toward the school again. I ended up standing at the same spot and contemplating some more. It had to be way past six o'clock. It was probably at least seven. The sun began to set, and I kept standing there until it was almost dark. What an awful feeling. I was afraid to miss out on a one-time opportunity, but the fear of going inside was even greater.

The effects from the alcohol were starting to fade, but I second guessed myself for too long to want to make an attempt. I started walking toward the entrance anyway, just for the heck of it. I thought that perhaps my intuition would allow me to enter, or maybe someone would notice me, and I would feel more comfortable.

As I walked up to the entrance, I was able to hear the joyful music that was being played, but there wasn't anyone near the door, so I went unnoticed. My instincts told me to just walk on by. Instead, I stopped underneath a large window, and I imagined what was going on in there. I had to take a look. It was eating me up.

The window was high off of the ground. I tried to jump a few times, but I couldn't get high enough to see anything. I jumped again and grabbed onto the outer ledge at the bottom of the window. I struggled to pull myself up, and I got high enough to take a peak.

Of course every time in the recent past that I played Tom taking a peep, I wished that I hadn't. There was the time when I caught Marty spitting on Patricia's sandwich. There was the time when I caught the two penguins kissing. There was the time I discovered Uncle Joe's nudie-man magazine, and, of course, there was the classic moment when I asked Cathy if I could take a peak under her skirt and Sister Theresa clobbered me, but I still didn't learn my lesson, so I took a good long look.

The lights were low, and slow music played. I recognized the song—Daddy's Home. About a dozen couples were dancing to it. I spotted Mike Santino taking a whirl with one of the girls. When he was making a turn, I saw that it was...Cathy! I kept watching as he lowered his hands down to her butt. Then I felt sick. I thought that I might puke the welfare wine out of my system while hanging in the air. I continued to punish myself as I kept watching, but I was losing my grip on the ledge. Then, I heard a loud voice yell, "Hey—what are you doing there."

I fell to the ground, hard. As I started to run, I felt like I twisted my ankle again, and then I definitely didn't feel like dancing anymore. To my luck, when I went back to school the following week, none of my classmates asked me why I wasn't there. Like everything else, I was able to dance my way around it.

The last big event for the month was the Easter candy sales contest. They decided to up the ante from the previous years. In the past, they would award prizes to the top three sellers. This year they would also give us a ten percent commission for everything that we sold. They were always thinking when it came to the dollars.

I figured that I would get my parents and grandparents to buy as much as possible because some of that would come back to me anyway. Then I would knock on all of the neighbor's doors. Everyone liked chocolate bunnies, or cream eggs, or jelly beans. I figured that selling a hundred dollars' worth should be a breeze…or maybe…two hundred?

Ratboy and I decided to make our rounds together. Of course, he had to get high on pot to build up his confidence to go knocking on the doors. Unfortunately, he talked me into it also. He didn't have to do much convincing. The drug was gradually becoming more comfortable inside of me.

I was off to a good start. I sold about thirty dollars' worth to my relatives the first day that I received the order forms. I got excited thinking that I was probably the top seller. Ratboy said that he was only able to sell a two dollar coconut egg to his family.

We decided to start at the end of my street near the top of the Layers. There were at least thirty houses on each side of my street. I picked the side that I thought I would get the best production. I based my theory on what I remembered from helping a friend with his paper route a few times. There were also a few nasty neighbors on the other side that I didn't want to deal with.

I still felt a bit weird after smoking the reefer, but I was sadly becoming used to that state of mind. Of course, I probably felt just as weird trying to sell candy to some of my neighbors the previous year when I was completely sober.

My first stop was at Mr. Sauters' house. He was a friendly old chap that I had many semi-enjoyable conversations with in the past. He would always share his worldly wisdom with me. He always looked dirt poor though, but I thought that maybe I could talk him out of a few bucks anyway.

I knocked on the door, and I could see through the window that he was trying to make an effort to answer my intrusion. He barely managed to get out of his chair, and then he carefully made his way to the door.

"Hi, Mr. Sauters, how are you doing?"

"What? …Who are you?"

"I'm Tom. I live down the street. You remember me…right?"

"Oh, ha-ha-ha, yea, what do you need, Ron?"

"No…uh…I'm…I wanted to know if you would like to buy some Easter candy from me?"

"Candy?" He started laughing again. "No, I don't have any teeth—see!"

"Oh! I'm sorry…I didn't know you didn't."

It was the ugliest mouth that I had ever seen. I didn't spot any teeth, and his gums were blackened. He could have had too much candy when he was a kid. He must have never brushed properly either.

"Why don't you come inside for a minute, John?"

I couldn't resist, but I wondered if he remembered who I was. As I walked inside I said, "It's Tom."

"Huh? What's that?"

"Nothing, Mr. Sauters."

I sat on his torn dirty couch. It smelled like cat piss. He started telling me his whole life story again. He talked in length about his childhood in Austria, or maybe he said Astoria. He didn't have much of an accent. He showed me every little relic that he had lying around. Then he pulled out some cash that he had sitting in an old coffee can. He wound up buying about ten dollars' worth for his grandchildren. I guess that my visit nearly paid off.

As I was leaving his house, I heard one of the neighbors screaming from across the street. "Get out of here—you little rat!"

I looked across the street—a few houses down, and I saw Ratboy running for his life. A woman with an angry look on her face came out to the sidewalk carrying a large broom. She was one of the neighbors that I didn't want to visit. There was a rumor going around that she practiced witchcraft. She looked like she wanted to beat him with the broom. As she walked back into her house, the witch yelled in disgust, "Little pissing thief! I'll burn down his britches!"

I thought that Ratboy probably wasn't the best salesman in town, but one way or the other, he was going to get paid. He stopped running once he got near the other end of the street. I was barely able to see him, but it looked like he went into another house.

By the time our knuckles got tired of knocking on wood, I had collected a total of ninety-nine dollars. Other than the egg that Ratboy sold to his parents, he sold two bags of jelly beans, but he still had a big wad of cash that rivaled mine.

The following week, our candy orders arrived at the school, and it was time to make my deliveries, but as usual, there was another dilemma. Because of my poor organizational skills and the pot that I smoked with Ratboy, I had all of my orders mixed up. I was too embarrassed to go around asking everyone to confirm their orders, so I decided to wing it. I had everyone's candy wrapped up and double bagged. By the time they would figure out what was what, I would be out of sight. Of course, most of my customers were either relatives or neighbors, so I probably wouldn't escape persecution completely.

I caught a break when I made my first stop at Mr. Sauters' house. When I knocked on the door, his next door neighbor was standing nearby. "He's not home now, kid."

I stood there contemplating whether I should leave the candy inside of his storm door. Then the neighbor lowered his voice. "He had a heart attack."

I didn't ask any questions. I just walked back home while toting his candy bag along with me. I sat in my house and contemplated for a few minutes. Then I dumped everything that I was going to deliver to him onto my kitchen table. I divvied up his candy with some of my other customer's orders. That way, even though I screwed everything up, I would be able to give something extra to some of my bigger customers. I kept a small white chocolate bunny as a reward for my smart thinking.

On Good Friday Sister Ann Margaret decided to have all of us go to the church for a morning mass. Then we would be excused early for the day. She also insisted that we would each meet with Father Murphy in the confession sweatbox.

While I waited in line, I was contemplating about how many of my sins that I wanted to reveal. It was almost April, and I figured that it might be my last good opportunity to repent for all of my evil doings while at Saint Luke. My time was growing tight, and I thought that it might be best to leave it all behind.

As I made my way into the box, I decided that I would tell Murphy everything: my sexual escapades, the pot smoking, the vandalism, the violence, but, then again, I didn't want him to have a heart attack like poor Mr. Sauters did.

As I hesitated, I could hear Father Murphy breathing on the other side. Then his gentle voice asked, "Can I help you?"

"Forgive me Father, for I have sinned. It has been…uh…a few…months since my last confession. I…uh…ch—cheated and I…uh…stole…uh…a white chocolate bunny…and…uh.…"

"Is that all, my son?"

I don't know why I told him I cheated…maybe I did on a test once, and who cared about the stupid bunny? I had a lot of real sins to confess, but I kept on hesitating.

"That's…uh…all I can think of now, Father. If I come up with anything else, I'll try to stop back later."

"Okay, recite three Hail Mary's and three Our Fathers."

"Thank you, Father."

As I got up from my kneeling position, Murphy said, "Oh, one more thing, Mr. Richards."

I was startled. I didn't realize that he knew it was me. I didn't think that he was supposed to know. I wondered if he was able to see me, or if he just recognized my voice. Either way, I felt that he was cheating the system. I was however, happy that I didn't reveal my entire portfolio of sins to him.

"Yes, Father."

"Keep an eye on your friend for me. Let's make sure that he stays on the path of righteousness."

He didn't have to tell me who he was referring to. I knew that he had seen Ratboy, and me together many times in the past. Of course, that same advice could have been directed to me, or the Santino boys, or Marty, or even Cathy for that matter.

"I will, Father...I will."

Then he finished by adding a little more responsibility onto my weak shoulders. "Remember—you are your brother's keeper."

I walked out knowing full well that I wasn't going to keep an eye on Ratboy anymore. It was our own responsibilities to keep an eye on ourselves. The brother's keeper comment sounded profound—like it was supposed to mean something to me but only briefly. Ratboy and I weren't even related. I also came to the conclusion that I enjoyed being a sinner, and I didn't want anyone keeping an eye on me either. I had become enchanted by the possibilities of sin...even on Good Friday.

Chapter Fifteen
Bye, Bye St. Luke

April was always a rainy month, but it seemed like we were getting more than usual. I could remember staring out the window on several occasions trying to determine if I could somehow walk around the raindrops without getting wet. I hated the constant downpours. I got a stomachache if I stared at it too long. I wanted it to stop. It made me think of my past too much. It made me think of my future way too much.

I didn't want to be that deep in thought about anything. I just wanted to live joyfully. I wanted to go out and soak up the sunshine. I didn't care if I became a genius inside the classroom, but I didn't want to flunk out, or be held back, or attend summer school like Ratboy either. Being a C+ student was just enough to keep everyone off of my back. I was a B- student before I got to the eighth grade.

On April twenty-third the rain decided to stop for a while. I stood in the yard during lunch time while eating a cheap chicken loaf sandwich. While I chomped away, I saw Marty chirping away to Mike and Tony. He looked like he was excited about something.

When he noticed me, he waved me over. I felt the anxiety of trouble brewing once again.

As I approached him, he shouted, "We're going over to Saint Mary's after school and kick they're asses!"

"How come?" I inquired.

"What do you mean—how come? Those pussies need their asses kicked! That faggot—John O'Reilly was mouthing off to me last weekend when I saw him down at the plaza. I'm going to punch a hole in his face. I'm going to shit on his head."

It was the most expressive and emotional words that I ever heard come out of the mouth of Marty Monday. The name John O'Reilly sounded familiar to me. Maybe it was his last name, because of the many Irish kids that attended Saint Luke. I think that he was one of the starters on their basketball team. They beat us both times that we squared off against them on the court over the past season. They were close games. That was probably part of Marty's furor. He was looking for a little payback.

I wasn't sure what to think. Maybe I needed to defend our reputation in the honor of Saint Luke, but did I really give a shit about honor or Saint Luke or Marty? I don't think I did.

Marty woke me from my deep thought when he said, "So, are you coming with us or what?

The three of them stared at me while waiting for an answer. I forced out the exact opposite of what I was thinking. "Yea, let's go down there and kick their pussy asses!"

During the afternoon session, for the first time in my life I prayed for more rain, but the heavens had nothing left to deliver. It was ideal fighting conditions. Since the weather wasn't cooperating with me, I wished that all of the clocks in the school would stop working or at least move a little slower, but two-thirty seemed to come awfully fast.

We decided to meet up outside of the White Front at fifteen-hundred hours. Marty was able to recruit Mike, Tony, Stanley Howard, Ratboy, his cousin Jimmy, and woe is me. It would be my first gang fight. With an exaggerated tone, Jimmy said, "This will be my third fucking fight this fucking year."

Jimmy was a fouled mouth ninth grader at Rockwood. You could tell that he had been around the block a few times. He had rugged features. He showed off his slick switchblade and said, "I plan on using this." He even had a cheap looking tattoo of a lion on his upper right arm, or maybe it was a bulldog. I forgot to ask him, and it was hard to tell. I thought that you had to be older to get a tattoo. Maybe it was a fakey. We all looked up to him anyway, and we unofficially made him the new leader…at least for the current mission.

So, seven little soldiers began their march to the battlefield.

***

Saint Mary's turf was on the other side of town. It was a good mile — at least a fifteen minute walk. We didn't know what to expect once we got there, but we played out the fight along the way. We would try to imitate Bruce Lee or Billy Jack. We would thrust our fist in the air and yell out a lot of filth which was motivated by Jimmy's well versed art of the bad language.

We knew that we were getting close when the Saint Mary's church steeple with the big clock came into view. Marty told O'Reilly that we would meet under the clock at three-thirty. It seemed odd to me that we would have a brawl in front of the church, but then I thought that perhaps we would be blessed and the fight wouldn't get too out of hand, and maybe there would be fewer casualties.

When we arrived at the front of the church and saw that nobody was there, Marty already claimed victory by yelling, "Those faggots chickened out."

Jimmy yelled, "I'll slice every one of those cock sucking, mother fucking, assholes!"

We all looked around to see if they were hiding, and I wondered if an ambush was in the cards. I started noticing how much nicer the houses and cars looked compared to the ones around my neighborhood. They definitely had more money than we did, and the kids always seemed more uppity. Perhaps they thought that we weren't worth their time and effort.

After standing around for a few minutes, Marty said, "Let's go up to the school."

Jimmy cleared his throat and held his hand in the air. I think that he wanted to call all of the shots. Without much hesitation he ordered, "Let's go up to the school, men. Let's take this hill!" He mentioned earlier that his uncle had also served in Vietnam.

The rest of us responded with more yelling, filthy language, and poor Kung Fu techniques. I noticed a woman who looked to be about a hundred years old was standing on her porch shaking her head. Then she went back into her house. Maybe, to call the cops.

We walked around the church and headed up the hill to their yard. There were more than a few kids assembled around the basketball hoop which looked a lot nicer and newer than the hoops on our turf. Actually, there were a lot of kids. As we got nearer, I started to count to myself…ten…fifteen…twenty…. I tried hard not to piss my pants.

The kid that was dribbling the ball noticed us and gestured to his friends. We were made, but we weren't going to back down after coming so far. We kept walking toward them, albeit at a slower pace as a bit of concern started to wash over all of us. Our loud battle cries had turned to almost whispers.

Marty said in a less than confident tone, "That's O'Reilly in the brown pants," while looking at Jimmy who was inspecting his switchblade.

We stood outside of the fence to their yard. None of us were feeling quite brave enough to cross over. We waited for them to make the first move. Our opponents stood around discussing their strategy for a minute. Then, O'Reilly started walking toward the fence with at least a dozen followers behind him.

He was holding on to a basketball when he yelled, "What do you punks want?"

We waited for Jimmy to say something, but he went mute, and his knife had conveniently slipped back into his pocket as he stepped back away from the fence.

Then Marty regained his tenaciousness. "I don't know. What do you want, fag?"

O'Reilly started to show anger in his expression. He bounced the ball once off the ground and then quickly off of Marty's face. I watched the ball as it rolled off of the sidewalk, onto the street, and down the hill. I eagerly wanted to follow its path.

Nothing else was said. I kept waiting for Fucking, Switchblade, Tattoo Jimmy to get involved. I waited for Big Bad Mike Santino to step up. I was waiting for Marty to return O'Reilly the favor. I didn't want to wait too much longer. I figured that if none of our three tough guys would make a rebellious move soon, then the best thing we could do was to steal their basketball.

O'Reilly surprised everyone by hopping over the fence, and he was quickly followed by most of his buddies. He didn't hesitate to crack Marty in the mouth…and again…and again! The rest of our gang stood there frozen, as did I. Then O'Reilly started to charge at Marty while trying to grab a hold of him. Marty slipped free and started to run. The rest of us instinctively followed him. I forgot about the basketball. I didn't feel like getting injured or killed.

We were outnumbered. We were outclassed. We were embarrassed while running away and listening to the Fairies from Saint Mary's yelling, "Pussies! Faggots! Go home!"

We didn't stop running until we got back to the White Front. Marty talked about regrouping and adding reinforcements, and then going back there. Nobody listened this time. Jimmy had quietly demoted himself, and he split the scene. Marty kept blabbing away while the rest of us started walking away from him. I used to despise Marty a little less back when he wasn't as talkative. The more he babbled, the more I wanted to get away from him. Eventually, he stood in front of the White Front all alone.

Later that evening the rain started coming down again. I thought that it would wash away the blood that was lost from the big brawl, except that there was only a tiny bit on Marty's face and on O'Malley's knuckles. There wouldn't be any evidence on the ground.

So, I went back to staring out the window and imagining how to maneuver around the raindrops again.

It took until the first week of May for the skies to dry out for more than a half a day. It was just in time for our blessed sacrament of Confirmation. I was hoping that the school had done away with it because it seemed like they hadn't performed the ceremony for a few years. It also felt like we were getting awfully old, and it was getting pretty late in the game for it to matter to most of us. I had to keep reminding myself that it was Holy Year, and Saint Luke wasn't going to let anything slip past him.

I didn't realize that four years earlier, the church had the fifth, sixth, seventh, and eighth graders confirmed all at once, and to save time and money, they would do it every four years instead of every two, which was formerly the tradition. They also wouldn't have to take up as much of the arrogant bishop's time, but he ended up sending a subordinate anyway—Father Francis. He was just a lowly pastor from another congregation. It made it all feel even less meaningful.

I felt like I was taking some type of hypocritical oath. The purpose of Confirmation was supposed to render our bond with the church more perfect. I didn't care to render, or bond, anything with the church. I even stopped getting Communion once we got past Easter. There was something about a priest saying body of Christ, and then dropping it on my tongue that was a real turnoff for me. I vowed that when my time was complete at Saint Luke, I would never return for any reason.

As I knelt and waited for my time to be confirmed, I imagined that Father Francis would somehow be able to see right through me. I even thought that he might turn me away. Would he know that I enjoyed being a sinner? Would he know that I wanted to have sex with every little Catholic girl, and maybe a few of the nuns along the way? Did he know that I would set my cassock on fire once I completed my final altar boy service? I guess that I was glad that it wasn't the bishop that was performing the service after all. Father Francis probably wasn't high enough up in spiritual rank to be aware that during my Confirmation…it was ironically my first step to becoming an atheist.

I first heard the term when one of the drunken, drug abusing degenerates that hung out at the Layers tried to explain to Ratboy and me that there was no proof that God existed. Then he ironically said "I do have proof that Satan exists though." The degenerate's unfitting nickname was Angel. He looked like he was about thirty years old, but he might have been only eighteen.

The gullible Ratboy asked, "How do you know that Satan exists?"

"Because…I'm him—that's why."

Then he reached into his coat pocket and pulled out a small can of lighter fluid. He squirted a good amount into his mouth. While his cheeks were puffed out, he lit a match in front of his mouth and out came a colossal ball of fire that went into the face of the unsuspecting Ratboy. Of course, I didn't believe that he was the devil, but I tried to keep my distance from that evil dragon from that day forward.

When I walked out of the church after Confirmation, I felt holy. It seemed like it was the end of one era and the start of another. I decided that it would be the last time I would step into the church. By doing that I also made a confirmed decision to retire from altar boy service while there were still a few weeks left in the school year.

On the final Saturday in May, it was time for our school picnic. Sister Ann Margaret said that because we were her all-time favorite class, and because it was Holy Year, the school would make sure that we would have a fun day that would provide us with the fondest of memories. Except for the Holy Year angle, I'm sure that she gave the same speech every year. Once again, I'm sure there were financial motivations.

The picnic would be at South View Park—home of the Lightning Bolt rollercoaster. It was certainly a step up from previous years. Sister Ann Margaret also told us that we had to buy our ride tickets from the school—a week in advance. I found out later that if I would have purchased my tickets directly at the park, it would have been much cheaper. What else is new?

As far as the fond memories, there were a few that would probably stand the test of time. Early in the day Ratboy threw up while riding on the Tilt-A-Whirl. The motion of the ride landed the vomit back into his face. When the ride was over, he stuck his repulsive head into the wishing pond to cleanse it. Then he jumped into the pond and cleaned out most of the coins that were tossed into it.

Throughout the day Cathy Davis let everyone have a turn with her through the Devil's Den. It was mostly dark inside the haunted ride and a good opportunity to feel her up. I noticed that Mike Santino took her inside a few times. I never asked her once. We had drifted apart by then.

The climax of the day was when I saw Marty Monday running through the park while being chased by three security guards. He knocked over some chubby woman in the process. The popcorn bag that she carried had spilled all over her and on the ground. A bunch of pigeons started to attack her for the free meal. Marty wasn't with us when we boarded the bus to go back home. Even though I was curious about what had happened, I didn't hear anything else about it.

***

Finally, it was June, and it was the last day of school. I didn't pay much attention to what anyone said or did for most of the day — except for when I saw Ratboy running out of the boy's room adjusting his trousers during lunch time. Sister Theresa came out after him. In disgust, she yelled, "You dirty little man! You filthy rat!" I guess that he finally got busted playing with his little monster.

Once again, I just kept watching the clock most of the day. When the final bell rang, I ran for the door. As soon as I got outside, I went into a chorus of Alice Cooper's other big hit—"School's Out". Mike, Marty, and Ratboy joined in. Then, after a round of slapping each other five, I walked out of the yard alone while ending the final chorus. I was finally finished with Saint Luke forever…completely… maybe?

Chapter Sixteen
September Ninety-Nine

Twenty-five years had gone by since the day I began my final year at Saint Luke. I had been thinking about it a lot lately. After all, it was the most memorable of all of my scholastic years. There were so many significant events that I experienced between September, Seventy-four and June, Seventy-five, that it set a course for the next quarter of a century.

I became a full-fledged atheist…I think. To play it safe, and because of a continuing fear of commitment, I would claim Agnosticism when those conversations surfaced, but I would still use expressions like Oh my god! My least favorite expression was always God bless you! Now seriously, if God existed, was I supposed to believe that he had such an intimate relationship with some mere mortals that he would recruit them to distribute his blessings? I usually felt like punching those distributors in the face. They were usually the same people that told me not to eat meat on Good Friday. I guess I had their assurance that even if I was a piece of shit the rest of the year, as long as I didn't eat a hamburger on that one day… I would be forgiven. If those fools were given the opportunity, they would have probably followed another fanatic to Jonestown for a drink of Kool-Aid.

I wouldn't step foot into a church, with the exception of the occasional wedding or funeral. It was over respect for the deceased or the committed but certainly not the church. However, I was always curious to see what the altar boys would have to do to perform those ceremonies, since I never got the opportunity.

At a recent funeral, I witnessed a friend of mine going up to the communion line with the rest of the zombies. I asked him afterwards, "What were you doing up there?" He looked embarrassed. He couldn't give me a good answer.

My grades continued to slip throughout high school, and I barely made it to the graduation pedestal. I gave college a try for a few semesters, but I just couldn't seem to fit in. I guess that I hated sitting in a classroom almost as much as kneeling in a church.

I also developed an annoying drug addiction through high school and beyond. I even became a small time dealer for a short period before I got busted. Fortunately, I was able to break away from the narcotics world by my thirtieth birthday.

I was almost married once, but that was before my fiancée — Mary busted me in a seedy motel room while I was having sex with two prostitutes on Good Friday. At least I didn't consume any meat that day. Mary was a good Catholic girl — a virgin. I should have known better.

I heard that the school had closed down several years back. I was curious to see if the old building was still standing where I left it. I also wanted to see if I was able to break away from whatever curse that Saint Luke had put upon me.

Just for fun I parked my car on Woodward Street—the street that I had lived on at the time, and I decided to foot the scenic route. I noticed that the old cobblestone was paved over with asphalt. I saw an old guy coming out of Mr. Sauters' house, but I didn't think it could be him. Nobody lives twenty-five years after having a heart attack, I reasoned. There was a resemblance. I thought that it might be his son.

I walked down the Layers, just like I did many years ago on my way to Saint Luke. The old wooden steps had been replaced by concrete. There weren't any degenerates hanging around. I noticed that someone made a foot impression on one of the steps before the concrete had settled, and next to the imprint they wrote Saint Luke Sucks.

I headed down Manicort Hill. It seemed a little bit steeper than I remembered, and the force of the wind seemed to be pushing me along at a brisk pace. I started to giggle like a thirteen year old—the way I may have way back then.

The hippie house was no longer there. It was probably condemned and torn down…or burnt down from the forces of hell!

Of course, there was no such thing as heaven or hell, but if there was a hell, the person in charge would have captured most of those damned hippies long ago…amongst others. I did understand that evil was all around us, and I made it a point to look at all of the faces in the crowd carefully…no matter their appearance.

It felt invigorating as I got closer to the school. I enjoyed every step of the way. I imagined that I saw my small footprints imbedded into the sidewalk. I tried to retrace the steps. It was difficult because my feet grew much larger and my stride became a lot longer than they were back then. I nearly tripped myself up, and I let out a loud laugh.

I started to have numerous flashbacks as I approached the schoolyard. It still looked mostly like I remembered it—except one of the basketball hoops was torn down, and the other three looked like they had barely survived with their rims severely bent and the backboards well deteriorated. Some of the asphalt was broken up from years of winter frost and pounding basketballs.

The building was still there, but it looked like a dinosaur. It appeared a lot darker and dingier than it did in its heyday. It also seemed smaller than I remembered. It kind of resembled an old, outdated rundown prison—like Alcatraz.

Judging by the boarded up doors and a few broken windows, it probably hadn't been in operation for a few years. I laughed again as I wondered if some other little punks thought that it was cool to throw some stones at the glass just like we did.

I stood there hoping that someone would have the same idea that I had, and we would have an unannounced reunion. We could shoot some hoops or play a game of handball. Maybe we could throw some stones at the windows again. We probably wouldn't get into any trouble. I wondered if anyone else ever streaked across the schoolyard.

I would have loved to see one familiar face, even if that person wore a habit. Of course, most of them were no longer around. Even if they were, we probably wouldn't recognize each other anyway. I just stood there trying to visualize some of the many faces.

There was one particular face that I couldn't get out of my head — the one that belonged to Ratboy. That's because we remained best friends for most of our lives. Then it got to the point where his lifestyle was getting too out of hand. I was trying to better myself, and we started to drift apart.

I ended up hearing from an old friend that Ratboy overdosed on blotter acid. It was about a month after his funeral when I eventually got the news, and I felt pretty sick about it. I remembered when Father Murphy told me to be my brother's keeper, and Chuck was the closest thing that I ever had to a brother.

I think that was the main reason why I came back to the school. I was an atheist that was looking for some sort of penance. I was told long ago that in times of crisis there was no such thing as an atheist in a foxhole. As I stood in the middle of the yard, an eerie feeling started to overcome me. I felt like Saint Luke was looking down on me and saying…so you decided to come back—sinner!

Chuck kept asking me for help, and I just kept ignoring him. He died in July, Nineteen Ninety-eight. Sometimes I would wake up in the middle of the night crying. On one particular night, I was so upset about it that I thought about the possibility of a deathbed conversion back into Christianity.

I wanted to get all of those depressing thoughts out of my head, and leave them where I was standing. I wanted them buried deep under the ground beneath me. I had a lot of nerve coming back to Saint Luke to search for some sort of salvation. I was just as perplexed standing there as I was a quarter of a century earlier.

I noticed that the skies above me were growing darker, and I heard a disturbing thunder in the distance. I looked up and saw a lively display of lightening at several places in the sky. It was a little unusual for as late in the year that it was. Then it started to drizzle, but I didn't want to leave just yet. I walked over to the entrance and stood beneath the awning for cover.

I immediately started thinking about the time Cathy Davis stood in front of me with an umbrella on the day that we had our first sexual romp at the side of the church. It was one of the more pleasant thoughts that I had…in a sinful sort of way.

I thought that maybe I should have taken her under my wings also. I was quite fond of her for a brief time, but we never had a formal relationship. She was just another girl that I wanted to have fun with. I think that perhaps she thought it was all any guy would ever want with her.

She seemed to have followed in her mom's footsteps. I heard that the two of them were hanging out together every night at the old Shamrock Inn. That was before the senior Mrs. Davis died of liver poisoning. Supposedly, Cathy is still a regular there, and she passes out blow jobs to support her crack habit. I drove past the Shamrock on a Saturday night a few months back, and I noticed that there was a long line of lowlifes waiting outside to get inside the bar. I imagined that Cathy sat at a corner table with a sign that read Fellatio for Five Dollars, and she went down on anyone with a crinkled fin.

The Santino brothers all seemed to conveniently follow in their father's footsteps. I witnessed Mike smashing a beer bottle over some unfortunate guy's head at one of the local bars when we were barely old enough to drink. A few years later, he ended up receiving a long stretch in the Southwestern Penitentiary for various wrong doings. I heard that he still conducts business from his cell. No institution or any punishment can deter crime.

Tony the prankster was also confined but in a slightly different setting. When he was in high school, I witnessed him beating his head on some of the hallway lockers on a few occasions. He eventually became a permanent resident in that happy little place called Willow Grove. I was told that he spends most of his free time picking his feces up off the ground and bouncing it off of the rubber walls, along with his head.

When Angelo Sr. had an untimely passing a few years back, the youngest son—Angelo Jr. took over the family empire. I've spotted him driving around town in his Cadillac Eldorado a few times. I heard numerous tales of drug dealing, prostitution, and bookmaking. It would be only a matter of time for him to get locked up also.

Marty Monday might have had the worst fate of all. He had all of the addictions: drugs, alcohol, gambling, sex, etc. He got himself into such a hole, that he turned to petty thievery. He decided to hold up a Stop-Go convenience store one night. He thought that he got away too—with a measly forty dollars. As he drove away from the scene, a bullet pierced through the driver's side window and into his neck. He crashed the car in front of a church and bled to death. As sad as it was, there was also something righteous about it. The store clerk that shot him was called a hero.

There were some success stories though. Calvin Gregory ended up getting elected to two terms as mayor of his small town. That was of course, before he got pulled over and charged with a DUI. It quickly ended his political ambitions, and then he ended up being a manager at the same Stop-Go convenience store that Marty robbed. He keeps a gun under the counter too.

Louis Selmon also used to have political ambitions. I remembered when I would always see him at Rockwood in the hallways or outside of the school with a group of kids standing around him. He always looked like he was giving an inspiring speech to them. He was taller than everyone else. By the time he was a senior, he looked like he was about six-foot-thirty. I often wondered if he ever regretted not playing basketball.

He ended up enlisting in the army, usually not a good move for a black kid. He must have figured that he would work his way up to becoming a General, and then it would be much easier for him to become President.

My cousin served in the Army around the same time and at the same base as Louis did. He said that Louis ended up getting dishonorably discharged, but he didn't know why. The last time I saw Louis, he was selling Kenmore appliances at the Allegheny Mall. He only attended Saint Luke for about half a school year, but that Old Catholic, black magic still must have rubbed off on him too. He decided to be just an ordinary person.

What about some of our glorious leaders at Saint Luke? I remembered reading in the newspaper recently that a Father Leonard Spencer was one of several priests that were indicted as part of a huge crackdown in the Boston area for sexual abuses within the Catholic Diocese.

In the end there were several multi-million dollar settlements with thousands of plaintiffs, and Spencer, along with many other holy terrors, were all defrocked permanently. There was no more shifting him around, no other places left to hide. It was too bad that Ratboy wasn't around to get his share. It could have been a lot more than he could have ever lifted from the poor box. He could have gotten some serious back pay…or pay back.

Uncle Joe retired from Saint Luke a few years after I graduated. He got to the point in his life that he no longer wanted to hide in his closet. I've seen him strolling around town a few times wearing a flaming red pair of leather pants. His shirts were also very colorful, as were the buddies that he hung around with. I wondered if he ever went into the confession box. My mom stopped inviting him to her house for the holidays.

I heard many other strange and depressing stories of some of the school's saints and sinners past. The most bizarre may be the one regarding Sister Mary Catherine. Rumor has it that after many years of service, she decided to kick the habit because she wanted to become a man. I heard that she moved up north and got a job working as a lumberjack in a logging camp, but the more I thought about it, from my memories of her, I started to believe every word of it, especially the lumberjack part…and the man part. I had no more desire to see her vagina anyway…if she ever had one.

I often wondered if any of the Saint Luke faculty was heterosexual or at least didn't have some sexual identity crisis. At least Mrs. Bun had a love-hate relationship with the other sex. My aunt knew her well. They were in the same grade at Saint Luke about twenty-five years before I attended. It was probably before the school became such a sin sanctuary.

Aunt Wilma told me that Bun was her second name change, and then she had three more husbands after that. Like a good Catholic girl, she divorced four of her men, and the fifth husband had mysteriously disappeared while they were on vacation in the Bahamas. With the insurance money and all of the alimony that she received, there was no need for her to work anymore. Soon after she retired from teaching, Mrs. — whatever her name was at the time had moved out of the country with all of her winnings.

After about an hour of reminiscing, the rain had stopped and the sky began to clear. I decided to walk away from the school for the last time and head back to my car. I didn't believe much in curses anyway, but I did have faith in fate.

As I walked through the schoolyard — at the other end, I saw a dark haired kid walking toward me while dribbling a basketball. As he got nearer to me, his face looked incredibly familiar. I thought that perhaps I was getting my wish after all, but how could that be? He looked like he was about…maybe thirteen years old? Did I travel back in time or something? Was it one of my déjà vu moments again? I hadn't smoked dope in a long time.

He had a cocky look to him—like he thought that he owned the place. As he walked past me, I couldn't help but ask, "Hey kid, do I know you from somewhere? You look so familiar to me."

He stared at me for a few seconds and said, "I don't know." He continued bouncing the ball toward the rusted hoop. Then he turned back toward me. "I'm Mike…Santino…maybe you know my dad."

I smiled for a few seconds. Then I shrugged my shoulders. "Oh…maybe not."

As I walked back to my car, I looked all around to see if any other faces would look familiar to me, or at least if they would remind me of someone from my past. Before I made it back to my old street, I walked past a kid that reminded me of a young Ratboy, and I saw a girl that seemed similar to little Cathy. They both looked so happy, and it made me feel better about the whole situation. Even though I had many painful memories, I desperately wanted the millennium to end on a good note.

I finally came to the conclusion that I was glad that I was still alive and reasonably intact. I was also happy that I wasn't confined, and I didn't feel that I had to thank Saint Luke or any imaginary god for anything. I realized that there were others that I knew that were given a worse fate, and things were starting to look up for me.

Considering everything, I felt like I was a survivor…well, at least for the time being.

www.ingramcontent.com/pod-product-compliance
Lightning Source LLC
Chambersburg PA
CBHW072049170626
46813GD00004B/128